ABOUT THE AUTHOR

Anthony Irvin studied veterinary medicine at Cambridge University, and after a period in UK farming practice, went to East Africa for two years and stayed for twenty where he became an expert on a disease of cattle and wildlife that no one outside Africa has ever heard of. He travelled widely through the region, worked closely with the Maasai and persuaded his bosses of the importance of establishing projects on the coast adjacent to the Indian Ocean, where, in between injecting cattle, he snorkelled among coral fish and stingrays, and windsurfed among sharks. He has also canoed among hippos, camped among elephants, climbed Africa's highest mountain, eaten crocodile, and photographed a rhino in his pyjamas. He now lives in wild Suffolk with his wife, two children and a collection of other animals, including a mischievously intelligent Parson Russell terrier called Tigger.

PRAISE FOR THE ANT-LION

I've just read The Ant-Lion and I have to say it was utterly fabulous. It was that good I would definitely buy all the next books in the series. The Ant-Lion is in my list of the best, most exciting books I've read! It had me sat reading it whenever I had some spare time. I can't wait to read your next books.

Samantha Salkus age 11

This was an excellent book. It made you just want to read on and on. The adventures were extraordinary and very exciting. The setting suited the story very, very well. It told me many facts about the Maasai people. It just makes me want to go to Africa again.

Tom Spetch age 10

The Ant Lion is a great book for Christmas gifts and I would give it to anyone from the age of eight to twelve. I am not the biggest fan of reading but I cannot wait for the next one to come out.

Ewan Evans age 12

The Ant-Lion was fantastic! It ticked all the right boxes. It was funny and the description was ace. The Ant-Lion had a really good story line to it and it flowed really well. Though I thought that it would be boring I was quick to change my mind. It was action-packed! The Ant-Lion had a great balance between funny and sad, action-packed and quiet. It told me lots of things about the African bush and wildlife. It made me want to be there. (I'm planning to start my begging soon!)

Fraser Park age 10

The Deemings

THE ELEPHANT-SHREW

Karibuni pwani - welcome to the coast

An African Safari Adventure

Tony

Anthony Irvin

Illustrations by Cat Sawyer
Cover Design by Catherine Duncumb

Matador
5 Weir Road
Kibworth Beauchamp
Leicester LE8 0LQ, UK
Tel: (+44) 116 279 2299
Email: books@troubador.co.uk
Web: www.troubador.co.uk/matador

ISBN 9781848764989

A Cataloguing-in-Publication (CIP) catalogue record for this book
is available from the British Library.

Printed in the UK by TJ international Ltd, Padstow, Cornwall

Matador is an imprint of Troubador Publishing Ltd

For CHRIS, SIMON and CLARE, safari drivers, cooks and naturalists.

ACKNOWLEDGEMENTS

While living and working in East Africa, I spent many weeks on safari in the bush and at the coast. My grateful thanks to those knowledgeable people who shared that passion, and from whom I learned so much about Africa, its remote places, its people and its spectacular wildlife, in particular: Ken Bock, Michael Gwynne, Robin Newson and their respective families. Special thanks to Subhash Morzaria, with whom I shared many coastal exploits on projects and windsurfers. I am especially grateful to colleagues who read and commented on numerous drafts and rewrites, particularly: Wilf Jones and David Axton, Carolyn Belcher, Pat and John Christie, Julian Corbell, Claire Frank, Ann Jessett, Sue Sawyer and George Wicker. My grateful thanks to Cat Sawyer and Catherine Duncumb who once again have applied their complementary artistic skills in portraying Africa and its animals so evocatively. Philip Daws of Waterstones has given the series his enthusiastic encouragement and support, for which I am greatly indebted. My thanks also to Bear Grylls for his most generous endorsement. My family, Susanna, Rebecca and Josh have once again tolerated my absentmindedness with patience and forbearance while I was engaged in writing, and have come to the rescue with perceptive thoughts and ideas at key moments; and Matt and Clare have helped beyond the call of duty. My final thanks are to Amy Cooke, Sarah Taylor and Jeremy Thompson at Matador for being so supportive, and for once more making the publication process not only painless but also pleasurable.

MAP OF TANZANIA

Showing main towns and features, and presumed location of Simba Ranch and Watumwani.

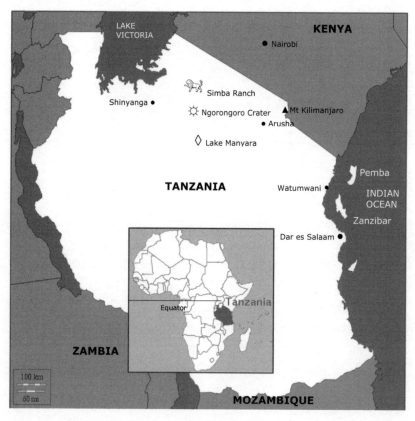

CHAPTER 1

Aardvark

A SCARY LANDING

Large drops like over-ripe plums splattered against the cockpit windscreen. In almost no time, the plane plunged into a torrent of rain that hammered and hissed with increasing ferocity and noise, until it drowned out even the sound of the engine. Lucy could see that Ellie's knuckles were white as she clung to the back of the seat in front of her; so was her face. Lucy's face was the same.

Craig was frowning, his jaw set tight.

Kal, who sat beside him in the co-pilot's seat, stared forward trying to see through the sheeting rain.

Beneath them, the ground had disappeared. They were now inside a waterfall – one that came straight at them.

Craig struggled with the controls but was powerless to stop the pounding torrent that had hit them without warning and which seemed determined to tear their tiny four-seater plane apart and hurl its occupants out of the sky.

Lucy felt sick and gripped her seat tighter. Fupi, Craig's terrier who was sitting on her lap, began to whine.

'It's all right, Fupi,' whispered Lucy. 'We're going to be okay.' She hoped she sounded more confident than she felt.

The last time she had flown this way, Mount Kilimanjaro was bright and clear, its snow-covered dome glinting in the sun. Now, all she could see as she peered over Craig's shoulder was rain streaming over the windscreen. She could barely make out the whirling propeller, and certainly not the mountain. For all she knew it could be directly in front. Kal, her thirteen-year-old brother, had told her that the plane flew at over a hundred miles an hour. They would have no warning.

Craig eased the plane lower.

At last, Lucy could see something: a rain-soaked landscape – totally featureless. But surely, that was something to their left. Craig had also seen it. Thank goodness – a road. He began to follow its line, then to Lucy's alarm, he handed the juddering controls to Kal, while he dug out a map and tried to identify it.

'We've just crossed into Tanzania,' he shouted, taking back the controls.

'Uh huh,' muttered Lucy. What did it matter? The only thing that mattered was surviving the ferocious storm.

The road turned sharp left and they had to leave it and carry straight on.

They were now flying beside a mountain – or what in the driving rain, Lucy took to be a mountain. Was it Mount Kilimanjaro or some other one? If there was a mountain in front it would hardly make a difference whether it was Kilimanjaro, the Ngorongoro crater (she knew that was nearby) or what it was, if they flew into it. She could imagine the newspapers: *"The holiday of a lifetime quickly turned to disaster for the Bartlett family when…"*

Craig wrenched back the controls and the plane shot upwards.

2

Lucy's stomach hit her feet. She and Ellie both screamed. Lucy had a brief glimpse of a rocky hillside through the driving rain. The plane shuddered. There was a crack like a gunshot and a branch whipped past her window. They had just flown through a tree!

Craig shouted something (it could have been the word Dad used when he hit the gatepost with their new car) and wrestled to bring the plane under control.

A few moments later, he turned to the girls. 'Sorry about that,' he shouted. 'We're okay,' he added, seeing their tear-stained faces.

Ellie grabbed the bag from the pocket of the seat in front and threw up.

Lucy clutched her nose and looked the other way, desperately trying to keep her own breakfast down. What was that, away to their left? She thought she could see a brighter patch. Craig turned towards it. They shot through a break in the clouds. The rain stopped as suddenly as it had started and they were into brilliant sunshine.

Lucy gave a great sigh of relief and her stomach began to settle.

Fupi wagged her tail. Lucy stroked her and began thinking about the Christmas holidays and their second visit to Simba ranch. Ellie, who was fourteen, had found it hard leaving behind television and Facebook to come to Africa for the first time on their previous visit, but was now looking forward to it as much as Lucy and Kal. They had arrived that morning from London with Dad. Mum was staying in the UK to finish some work and would be flying out a week later in time for Christmas. Craig, who was Mum's cousin, had met them at Nairobi airport in Kenya, and they had taken Dad to the university where he would be acting professor of geology. Imagine, Dad a professor! Lucy didn't think he looked much like a professor – not that she'd ever met one – he didn't have enough hair. Now, they were on their way to Simba, the wildlife conservation ranch that Craig managed in Tanzania. Lucy couldn't wait to...

The engine coughed and the plane lurched. Then another cough.

Craig looked anxiously around and turned towards a tiny patch of ground without any trees – at least, not big ones. Lucy was horrified. Surely, he wasn't going to try and land on something no bigger than their back garden.

The engine gave another cough.

'No-o-o,' wailed Lucy, and shut her eyes. Fupi licked her face. 'Say your prayers, Fupi,' she whispered.

Another splutter from the engine – then silence.

Lucy had just had her twelfth birthday. Was it to be her last? She wondered if she would meet her deceased hamster on the other side. She could hear Ellie whimpering.

There was a bump. Lucy's eyes flew open. Bushes raced past outside her window. Another bump. Then the plane's wheels were rolling along *on the ground*. There was a sharp crack. The plane slewed round, and stopped.

'Can we do that again, please, Craig?' said Lucy, then passed out.

❦

The next thing Lucy knew, she was lying on the ground and Craig was looking into her face, his eyes full of concern.

'Are you all right, Lucy?'

'Yeah, no sweat,' she said, mimicking one of his favourite phrases.

He grinned. 'Some landing, hey?'

She sat up and looked around. Kal was examining the plane and Ellie sat with her back to a tree staring into space. Fupi lay beside Lucy, her ears back, her nose resting on her paws and her eyes also staring into space.

'Well done, you lot, for not panicking,' said Craig.

'Speak for yourself,' muttered Ellie.

Craig went to the plane and returned with a thermos. He poured some hot coffee into a cup. 'There, drink that.'

Ellie took the cup without a word and sipped the contents. She looked up and gave a weak smile. 'Thanks, Craig.'

'Good on you.' He smiled back, and poured out a cup for each of them.

Lucy hated coffee – but not today.

'That was a bit hairy,' said Kal.

'Hairy scary,' agreed Lucy.

Craig pulled a face and turned to Kal. 'What's the damage, skipper?'

'One of the port-side struts between the wing and the undercarriage is bust,' said Kal. 'That's what slewed us round, and there's some crud in the air intakes – probably leaves.'

'I'm afraid that tree came up rather quickly,' said Craig, 'but it doesn't sound too serious.'

'Not serious!' cried Ellie. 'You're surely not thinking of flying in *that*. It looks like a dead… a dead dodo!'

'It's either that or a long walk.'

'Can't you call up someone on the radio and tell them to come and meet us?' asked Lucy.

'Ah,' said Craig. 'That's the bit I didn't tell you.'

'You don't mean the radio's broken?' cried Ellie.

'Afraid so. It got bashed. And my mobile's back in the office,' he added.

'What are we going to do?' Ellie's lower lip began to tremble.

'Listen, guys,' said Craig. 'The most important thing is we're safe, and no one is injured. Secondly, we've got plenty of food, water and supplies…'

'Are we spending the night here?' asked Kal.

'No choice. It'll take several hours to fix things,' said Craig, 'and we've got to clear some bush to make a take-off strip – that'll also take time.'

'Cool,' said Kal.

Ellie folded her arms across her body and glared at Craig. 'It may be cool for Kal but I'm afraid I haven't done aircraft maintenance and runway construction,' she snapped. 'They somehow got missed off our school curriculum.'

Craig grinned. 'Kal and I can sort that.'

'So what do Lucy and I do – weave blankets and build grass huts?'

'If you like.'

Ellie snorted, then her mouth crinkled. 'Craig, you're impossible!' She tried to stop herself laughing, but it was no good. Lucy and Kal joined in.

Craig's grin widened. 'See that compartment at the back of the plane?'

Ellie nodded.

'You girls get the gear out. Find what we've got, then see about setting up camp and getting some food together.'

Lucy and Ellie found a box containing cooking utensils, blankets, matches, mosquito nets, torches and some bottles of water. Lucy rummaged further and found corned beef, biscuits, dried milk, flour, tea, sugar and dried fruit. Craig was obviously prepared for emergencies, but knowing him she wouldn't have expected any less.

'Over there.' Craig pointed to a cliff-face that they could just make out through the trees. 'That should have given some shelter from the rain. Let's see if we can find somewhere dry.' He led them through the bush.

'Look!' cried Kal, as they approached the cliff.

Ellie grabbed Craig's arm. 'What is it?' she whispered.

'There.' Kal pointed.

'It looks like some sort of cave,' said Lucy.

'Could be,' said Craig. 'Let's see.'

Ellie hastily released Craig's arm and looked embarrassed. 'Don't leopards live in caves?'

'Sometimes,' said Craig.

Fupi approached the entrance, her nose and ears straining forward. Craig threw a stone into the cave. It echoed with a hollow ring. Fupi barked. Craig threw another. Nothing happened – except the echo. He stuck his head into the entrance and sniffed.

'Bats, I guess, but no leopards. Look, and no tracks in the sand.'

'That *is* a pity!' muttered Ellie. 'I was looking forward to being disembowelled.'

'Leopards go for the neck,' said Kal. 'You wouldn't feel a thing.'

'Hey, knock it off!' cried Craig. 'You're making me nervous. Come on, let's check it out.'

'I'll get the torches,' said Kal. He ran back to the plane, returning a few minutes later. He passed one of the torches to Craig then followed him into the cave. Lucy was beginning to wish she'd stayed outside with Ellie. It wasn't much fun crawling into the darkness, with only wavering torchlight in front and a strange musty smell that was getting stronger. There was a fluttering and a large golden something shot out into the light and disappeared into the trees.

Lucy squawked. 'What kind of bird was *that*?'

'Yellow-winged bat,' came Craig's muffled voice. 'They sometimes roost in caves.'

'But it was enormous!'

'Sabre-toothed vampire,' said Kal. 'They also go for the neck.'

'Rubbish!' said Lucy, hoping she was right.

'Hey, it opens right out,' called Craig.

Lucy scrambled forward. Craig and Kal were standing up and shining their torches round the inside of a large and roomy cave.

'It's fantastic!' cried Lucy, as she joined them. 'Bit pongy, though.'

'That's the bats,' said Craig. 'See, up there.' He shone his torch into the roof of the cave, and Lucy could make out a dark restless mass of tiny bodies.

'There's millions of them! But they're not yellow.'

'Different species,' said Craig.

'Oh.'

Fupi trotted round sniffing. Kal followed her with his torch. 'This would be a great place to have a camp.'

'Why not?' said Craig. 'Others have.' He shone his torch onto the remains of a fire that Fupi was now inspecting. 'It's warm and dry, and if we light a fire in the entrance nothing will disturb us.'

'I'm not sure I want to sleep with all those bats above me,' said Lucy.

'They'll go out to hunt as soon as it gets dark,' said Craig. 'Come on, let's get sorted.'

They fetched their things from the plane, found a flat area in the cave and spread out what bedding there was. They would use their bags as pillows. It would be an uncomfortable night but certainly better than sleeping in the open.

Kal helped Craig to get a fire going outside then Ellie and Lucy cooked supper. It was a bit of a disaster but no one minded. They certainly felt full after eating Ellie's *corned beef surprise* (chunks of corned beef fried in lumpy flour), accompanied by soggy chapattis. Afterwards, they ate some berries from a bush that Kal reminded them was called 'snot-berry'. Trust him to remember *that*, thought Lucy.

When they had finished, they sat warming themselves by the glowing fire and tried not to think about their near disaster as they watched the sparks rise and mingle with the twinkling stars overhead.

'Here they come!' cried Lucy.

Bats were flying out of the cave. At first there were a few, but they quickly became a swarm and the air was filled with the sound of rustling wings as the emerging bats flew a few circuits above their heads then tore off into the gathering dusk.

'There really *are* millions!'

'We'll give them half an hour or so,' said Craig, 'then we'll move in.'

'Craig, who else do you think has used the cave?' asked Lucy.

'Would it be poachers?' asked Kal. 'There were the remains of a fire.'

'Could be,' said Craig, 'hunters of some sort, I guess.'

'Will they come back tonight?' asked Ellie.

'No chance,' said Craig. 'If there are any in the area, which I doubt, they'll want to keep well clear of us.'

'I reckon cavemen lived here thousands of years ago,' said Lucy. 'Just think: they could have been sitting round a fire like us, watching bats and eating mammoth or chewing bones. Cavemen, then Egyptians, then Romans, then Arabs, then Europeans. They've all slept in the cave at sometime or another. Think of all that history.'

'Sounds like the League of Nations,' said Craig, chuckling.

'Sounds like a load of rubbish,' said Kal.

'All right,' said Lucy, '*be* unromantic! But I bet some have.'

'Certainly Arabs,' said Craig. 'Arab slave traders came all through this region, and not much more than a hundred and fifty years ago.'

'So perhaps that's a slave trader's fire,' said Lucy, in a spooky voice. 'He probably had all his slaves shackled to a tree.' She pointed. 'There, that one. I bet that's the one.'

Craig laughed.

'But it could be true, Craig, couldn't it?'

'I guess it could, Lucy,' he said, standing up and stretching. 'Come on, guys, time for bed. Kal, give me a hand. We'll need to… Shh!'

'What is it?' whispered Ellie in alarm.

Craig shone his torch. 'Look – over there.'

The light picked out a large animal like a pig with pointy ears and a long snout and tail, bumbling between the bushes and snuffling into holes and crevices.

Ellie gasped. 'What is it?'

'It's an aardvark!' squeaked Lucy.

The animal stopped and peered short-sightedly in their direction then turned its attention to a large termite mound that it ripped into with powerful claws, grunting as it did so.

'These guys are so strong,' whispered Craig, 'that stuff's like concrete. But see, he's already broken in.'

They could hear slurping sounds as the aardvark sucked up termites by the bucketful.

'Sounds like Dad with his porridge,' murmured Kal.

Lucy snorted.

The aardvark looked up then scampered off into the night.

'That one could disembowel you,' said Kal.

'Just shut up, will you!' snapped Ellie. 'We will be safe won't we, Craig?'

'Sure. Those guys don't go in caves – they dig their own holes. Come on.'

He and Kal pulled a log out of the fire and dragged it in front of the cave entrance. It took them only a few moments to prepare for bed; they simply lay down on the sparse bedding and turned out the torches.

As Lucy's eyes adjusted to the dark, she could see occasional flickering from the burning log outside. People have lived like this for thousands of years, she thought. Despite the hardness of the ground, she found it really cosy. Fupi was snuggled against her. Already, she could hear Kal snoring. To think: cavemen, and Egyptians, and Romans, and... She was asleep.

Ellie couldn't sleep. She kept turning over trying to get comfortable on the uneven ground, and she couldn't stop thinking about all the people who might have used the cave. Perhaps people have died in here trying to escape from wild animals or slave traders. Perhaps it's haunted.

And what about animals – leopards and aardvarks? She remembered what Kal had said: "*Leopards go for the neck. You wouldn't feel a thing.*" That's probably just one of his made-up stories. But she couldn't put it out of her mind. And what about aardvarks? Did they really stay away from caves, like Craig said? She could still picture those powerful claws ripping into the termite mound. Perhaps this aardvark was different from normal ones. Perhaps it was just waiting until they were all asleep, then it would come into the cave, its long nose snuffling after them, its powerful claws ready to...

Go to sleep.

From where she lay, she could see the opening and the flickering log outside. Every so often it would flare up and send ghostly shadows round the inside of the cave. She turned over and closed her eyes. She turned back and opened them again. The log still flickered and the ghostly shadows still stalked round the cave. But *that* wasn't a shadow. The hairs rose on the back of her neck. What was it? It was only a silhouette, but...

She tried to scream but no sound came out.

CHAPTER 2

White-tailed mongoose

NIGHT-TIME VISITOR

Ellie grabbed Craig and shook him.

He was awake in an instant. 'What is it, Ellie?'

She couldn't speak. All she could do was make choking noises. She pointed. 'There… something,' she blurted.

'Where?'

'Something… someone, looking at us.'

'Ellie, I can't see anything.'

'Look! There… It's… it's gone.'

'What was it?' Craig gave her arm a reassuring squeeze and her pounding heart began to settle.

Kal gave a loud snore, and Lucy muttered something in her sleep.

'Craig, something or someone was outside peering into the cave.'

Craig shone the torch. 'Ellie, there's nothing there.'

'There was. It may have gone now but there *was* something.'

Fupi had been woken and was trotting round the cave sniffing. Craig followed her with the torchlight.

'What sort of thing, Ellie? A person, an animal, what?'

'I don't know, but it was big.'

'How big?'

'Quite... Craig, I don't know,' she whimpered.

Fupi trotted back to Craig and wagged her tail.

'See, Fupi's not worried,' he said.

Ellie reached out and stroked the little dog. Fupi licked her hand and nestled against her.

Craig checked his watch. 'Ellie, it's one in the morning. Try and get some sleep.'

'Sorry, Craig, but it looked so real.'

'The shadows can play funny tricks with your eyes.'

'I suppose so.'

'Try not to worry. Fupi will warn us if anything comes.'

Ellie stroked Fupi again and put her arm round her.

Kal gave another snore.

◦≈◦

When Lucy woke next morning, she could see it was light outside. She lay waiting for her eyes to accustom to the small amount of daylight seeping into the cave. Ellie was still asleep but Craig and Kal had already left.

Fupi stood up, stretched, yawned, wagged her tail, gave Lucy a lick and trotted out of the cave. Lucy followed.

Craig and Kal were sitting by the fire warming their hands while they waited for the kettle to boil.

'How did you sleep, Lucy?' asked Craig.

'I don't remember a thing.'

'You weren't disturbed by our visitor, then?'

'What visitor?'

'Come.' Craig led her back to the mouth of the cave and pointed to some tracks in the sand. Fupi sniffed them suspiciously.

Ellie emerged looking dishevelled.

'I guess I owe you an apology,' said Craig, pointing at the tracks.

Ellie gave a gasp. 'I knew I'd seen something. Is it the aardvark?'

Craig shook his head.

'A leopard?'

'No, the prints are too small. I reckon they're white-tailed mongoose,' he said. 'That's the big one.'

'I said it was big.'

'Looks like it went into the cave,' said Kal.

Although their own tracks had obliterated most of the mongoose footprints, they could still see one or two imprints that clearly led inside.

'So much for burning logs to keep intruders away,' sniffed Ellie.

'You could have been eaten alive,' said Kal.

'Shut up!'

Craig smiled. 'There'll be plenty of beetles, mice, and things in the cave; that's probably what it was looking for.'

'Do you mean, I've been sleeping with those things crawling all over me?' cried Ellie. 'I wouldn't have slept a wink if I'd known.'

Craig grinned. 'That's why I didn't tell you.'

'Honestly!'

No one could face *corned beef surprise* for breakfast but Ellie found some digestive biscuits, dried mango and a tin of sardines.

Lucy gave Fupi the remains of last night's supper and it disappeared in a moment.

'That'll give her stomach something to grip on when we're in the plane and she throws up,' said Kal.

'Kal, that's disgusting!' cried Lucy. 'Anyway, Fupi's not like that.'

'Craig,' said Ellie, as she munched her unusual breakfast, 'if it was a mongoose in the cave last night, how come Fupi didn't smell it?'

'Kal's feet?' suggested Lucy.

Craig smiled. 'Fupi would have known but she also knows a mongoose is not a problem.'

'Fupi, you're very clever,' said Lucy, tickling Fupi behind the ears.

Fupi wagged her tail and watched to see if Lucy would drop a bit more sardine.

~~◈~~

They cleared up the breakfast things – a knife and a tin opener – then went back in the cave to pack up the bedding and their bags. Kal was the first to finish and went looking for the mongoose tracks.

'Come here,' he whispered. He bent down and shone the torch into a crack deep in the back of the cave.

Fupi strained forward and sniffed, her tail between her legs.

'There's something in there,' whispered Kal.

The others crowded round and could make out the shape of an animal. It was brownish grey, and had a large white bushy tail that it had wrapped round itself. It was sound asleep. Lucy could see its body rising and falling with its breathing.

'Is it a white-tailed mongoose?' she asked.

'Yes,' said Craig.

Lucy knelt down to peer closer then gave a squeak. 'Look! I can see two little tails. It's got babies!'

15

'So that's why,' whispered Craig. 'She had probably been out hunting when we moved in and was afraid to return until we were quiet. Come on, we'll leave her in peace.'

They tiptoed away.

'Let's see what other surprises there are,' said Lucy. 'This is such a brilliant place, I'm sure there'll be treasure hidden somewhere.' She shone the torch slowly round the cave. 'The bats are back,' she said, shining the light into a dark rustling mass on the roof. 'Now, let's see, where would the Arab slave-trader hide his treasure?'

'What you need,' said Kal, 'is a map with a large X marked in the middle.'

'You can tease,' said Lucy, 'but this is just the sort of place where people do hide gold and jewels and things – like in books.'

'Dream on,' said Kal, flashing his torch aimlessly round the cave. 'There you are then, Lucy, there's the secret code that'll lead you to the treasure.' The light was shining on some squiggles that had been scratched on the wall. 'Only problem is reading it,' he said, and moved the light on.

'Kal, wait!' cried Ellie. 'Shine the torch back where you were.'

'Just scribbles – some kid messing about.'

'Kal, keep the torch still,' said Ellie. She peered closely at the marks. 'No, it's writing; I'm sure it is. Has anyone got a paper and pencil? I'm going to copy this down.'

'Here.' Craig passed her a notebook and pencil from the pocket of his shirt.

'It certainly looks like writing,' murmured Ellie, as she scribbled away.

'What sort?' asked Lucy.

'I don't know but I suppose it could be Arabic.'

'That would figure,' said Craig.

'There, I told you!' cried Lucy triumphantly. 'I told you an

Arab slave trader had slept here. It's a message telling us where he's hidden his loot.'

'Rubbish,' said Kal. 'It probably just says, Ali Baba slept here.'

Some of the squiggles were quite faint, and Ellie had to be very careful to copy their exact shape and the dots and other small marks.

'What do you think, Craig?' asked Lucy.

'It certainly looks like writing, and Arabic is the most likely.'

'I bet it's old,' said Lucy.

'Could be,' said Craig. 'There's no weathering of the rock inside this cave, so there's nothing to wear the marks away. Also, it's probably ages since any Arabs passed this way and slept in caves. Any that come by nowadays are usually driving Mercedes and staying at fancy lodges.'

'Let's see if there's any more,' said Kal. He started systematically shining his torch up and down the walls of the cave, and although they searched for nearly half an hour, they failed to find anything else that looked remotely like writing, although they did find some scratch marks that Craig said were probably made by a leopard.

'What we have to do now, is get this translated,' said Ellie.

'What we have to do now,' said Craig, ' is get away from this place.'

∽৵ঔৎ৹

As they packed everything back into the plane, Lucy looked apprehensively at the bits of seat frame that Craig had riveted to the undercarriage. It looked strong enough, but... She didn't like to think about it.

Craig brought out two *pangas* – machetes – from inside the plane. 'We'll take turns.' He passed one to Kal and kept the other for himself. 'We've got to clear the bush from here to about where that termite mound is,' he said, pointing. 'You girls check out the rest of the strip and remove any branches or rocks, and see if there are any holes.' He and Kal began chopping away grass tufts and clearing bushes.

The children took turns with the *panga*, but Craig just kept going. Gradually, the semblance of a track emerged but Lucy didn't think it looked remotely like the sort of place you would use to take off in a plane. She was distracted by sudden barking and hurried over to Fupi. 'Craig, there's a massive hole here,' she called, 'right in the middle of the track.'

They peered into it. Fupi started to go down, her tail wagging furiously.

'No!' cried Lucy. She grabbed one of Fupi's back legs and hauled her out.

'See if you can hear anything, Lucy,' said Craig. 'Stick your head down.'

'And get it bitten off!'

'No, it's quite safe,' said Craig grinning.

'*Quite* safe. What's that supposed to mean?'

'Go on, try.'

Lucy cautiously lowered her head nearer the hole. 'It pongs a bit.'

'Can you hear anything?'

'No – yes!' she cried. 'It sounds like Kal.'

Craig laughed.

'Here, let me listen.' Kal pushed Lucy aside and stuck his head into the hole. He emerged a moment later, a big smile on his face. 'Not me – Ellie.'

'Mind, Kal', said Ellie. 'I suppose muggins will be the one who gets eaten.' She knelt down beside the hole and listened. Then she lifted her head. 'Lucy was right, just like Kal. Is it a hyena?'

'Hey, watch it!' cried Kal.

Craig shook his head. 'What do you think, Lucy?'

'Is it the aardvark?'

Craig put his head down to the hole. 'That's him, snoring his socks off. He's set for the rest of the day – probably tired after all his 'ard wark in the night.'

'Craig, that's a terrible joke!' cried Ellie.

'Sorry.'

'We can't fill in his hole,' said Lucy, 'he'd suffocate.'

'Not much chance of that,' said Craig, 'but we won't disturb him.' He went and cut a leafy branch, which he stuck into the hole. 'I'll be able to see that.'

Ellie and Lucy exchanged anxious glances.

'Road works ahead,' said Kal.

Ellie looked back along the strip they had cleared and put her hands on her hips. 'This is madness!' she cried. 'Not only are we going to try and take off in the middle of a ploughed field but we're now adding some road works just to make it more interesting. I'd rather do free-fall parachuting.'

'You may have to,' said Kal.

She glowered at him. 'That, Kal, was not funny.'

The sun disappeared behind a cloud.

Craig glanced up at the sky. 'Come on, guys, we need to move it.' He hurried them back to the plane.

As they scrambled aboard, Lucy looked with alarm at the thickening cloud. She and Ellie sat on the floor, and strapped themselves in as best they could.

Craig closed the doors, started the engine and turned to them. 'Okay?' he mouthed, above the noise.

They nodded uncertainly.

Craig winked at them and turned back to the controls.

Lucy looked out of the window. Spurts of sand were popping up where great drops of rain were falling. Outside was now even darker. The engine noise increased and she could feel the plane trembling like a nervous horse trying to break loose. If Craig revved much more it could fall apart. She held tightly to Fupi.

Craig released the brake and they started to speed forward.

Lucy was too low down to see out of the front, but she could feel the plane bumping over the rough ground and could imagine the aardvark's hole racing towards them. The next thing she would know would be the plane somersaulting then…

Then they were up.

The bumping stopped, the rain stopped, and they flew into the sunshine.

Twenty minutes later, Simba Ranch came into view. Lucy could see the main house, and there were the animal pens, and that was the house where Samson and Martha lived. And that figure running from the animal pens to the main house must be Matata, their adopted son. She saw other figures appear, look up and wave to them. Then she lost sight of them as Craig lined up for landing. She felt the wheels bump onto the ground and run smoothly over its surface.

The plane coasted to a gentle halt. Lucy was about to release her belt, when the plane gave a groan and sank onto its side.

Craig turned off the engine. 'Welcome back to Simba.'

Even if the plane wasn't in one piece, they were.

CHAPTER 3

Silver-backed jackal

FUPI TO THE RESCUE

The short rains, which should have ended by October, hadn't; they had simply continued. As soon as everyone was out of the plane, the rain started again and by the time they reached the vehicle that was waiting for them, they were soaked. So was Samson, the assistant manager at Simba, who greeted each of them in turn. 'It is good you are safe,' he said. 'Diana was very worried. We were all worried.'

'So were we,' muttered Ellie.

They threw their bags into the vehicle and scrambled aboard.

'Can I drive?' asked Kal.

'You haven't forgotten?' said Samson.

'No way!'

Samson laughed.

The stone bungalow with the veranda running along one side

was just as Lucy remembered. Standing there out of the rain, were Diana (Craig's mother), and Martha (Samson's wife), who was the housekeeper. But the Maasai boy, holding the football and waving like mad, was not in the least troubled by the rain.

Kal stopped the vehicle, and Matata came running up.

'*Karibuni, karibuni* – welcome, welcome!' he cried, in great excitement, coming and shaking everyone's hand – including Samson's, whom he had seen only a few minutes earlier.

'Now I speak English very good,' he said, but then reverted to Swahili.

Lucy could recognise only the odd word, but Ellie clearly hadn't forgotten any of her Swahili.

'What's he saying?' asked Lucy.

'He's asking us how we are, whether we had a good journey, about Mum and Dad, how things are at home, and if the cows are well.'

'The cows! But we don't have any cows.'

'Of course we don't but Matata doesn't know that. He thinks because we're rich…'

'I wish,' said Lucy.

'We are by his standards. He thinks because of that, we must own lots of cattle.'

'And keep them in the spare room, I suppose.'

'Lucy!'

'Sorry. Just thinking about all that mucking out.'

'You'd have to chuck it out of the window,' said Kal. 'Mum would never let you take the barrow up and down the stairs now we've had a new carpet fitted.'

'We might have to put it all in bags and…'

'Stop it, you two!' cried Ellie. 'You have to realise that Matata has no idea how we live; he only knows the ranch and the immediate area. He knows nothing about England. And Shinyanga is probably the only town he knows.'

'That's not much like Putney,' said Kal.

'I know that, but Matata doesn't.'

'He looks really well,' said Lucy, watching Matata who was now racing over from the Land Rover clutching an armful of bags and then racing back again. What a change from the time they had found him living alone in the forest, when he was thin and dirty and had a horrible sore on his leg, and above all, was terrified. Lucy was so glad that Martha and Samson, who had no children of their own, had adopted him.

Having changed into dry clothes, the children and Craig were back on the veranda having lunch. There was much oohing and tutting as they recounted their adventures, and learned how Samson had been in touch with the police and how Diana had contacted the hospitals in Arusha and Shinyanga.

Lucy only half listened as she stroked Fupi who was sitting on her lap. She was remembering everything about Simba and how she had missed Africa. But now she was back and it was just so brilliant. She wondered how many new birds she could add to the list she'd made on their previous visit.

'Look!' cried Ellie. 'It's stopped raining.'

'And here's the sun,' said Diana.

'Come on, Fupi,' said Lucy, 'we're going to the animal pens.'

She and Fupi ran round to the back of the main house. Joel, Simba's game scout, who was in charge of the orphan animals, was leaning on the fence of one of the pens, watching a young eland and a dik-dik that were nibbling some fresh leaves.

'*Jambo*, Lucy,' he cried. 'How are you since many days?'

'*Jambo*, Joel, it's so good to be back. How are you?'

'Fine.' He shook her hand. 'See, they are pleased to see you.'

'Caspar, Pofu,' she called. The two animals came and poked their noses through the fence and sniffed her hand.

'Come,' said Joel. He opened the gate of the pen and led Lucy in.

'Caspar,' she called, 'come here.' She knelt down and the little dik-dik trotted up and put his whiffly nose into her hand. 'It's so nice to see you again,' she murmured, stroking his smooth glossy coat. 'You look so well.'

'And see his leg,' said Joel, 'it is very better.'

Lucy felt the place where Caspar's leg had been broken when they first found him. She could still feel a slight lump but the leg was straight and Caspar showed no sign of pain or lameness.

The eland came and butted Lucy in the back, nearly pushing her over. She laughed. 'All right, Pofu, so you want a stroke as well, do you?' She stood up and rubbed the eland's neck. She couldn't believe how much he'd grown.

'Every day now, we take them for walking,' said Joel. 'Soon they will be ready to leave.'

Lucy felt sad. She knew that the animals had to be released back to the wild as soon as they were old enough, but she wondered if she could bring herself to do it – particularly with Caspar. Or would Craig insist?

She looked around the pen. 'Joel,' she cried, pointing to a small shelter at the back, 'another dik-dik!'

Joel smiled. 'That one is a lady. Matata found her when her mother was killed by a hyena.'

'That's awful!' Lucy held out her hand and called softly. Although the little dik-dik opened her eyes and looked at her, she didn't move, just whiffled her nose in Lucy's direction. 'She's beautiful, Joel. What's her name?'

'We wait for you, Lucy.'

'You want *me* to think of a name?' Lucy furrowed her brow. What would be a good name?

'Come,' said Joel, 'there is another one who wants to see you.' He led Lucy to an enclosed pen set away from the others. A beautiful spotted animal was running back and forth making excited "*how how*" noises.

'Mondo!' cried Lucy. She ran up to the pen and the serval came and rubbed itself against the bars. Lucy reached through and rubbed his soft ears.

'He also is now better,' said Joel. 'And there is no sign of a wound.'

Lucy felt the animal's flank where she and Craig had sewn up the skin. 'You so nearly died,' she murmured, remembering how Mondo had arrived in a sack, having been speared by some children who thought he might attack their goats. 'You are so beautiful.'

'Come, Lucy, now is the time for walking,' said Joel. He led her back to the other pens and began calling out names as he let out the respective animals. There was a young zebra, three warthogs, a bushbuck, Pofu the eland and Caspar. They all followed Joel as he continued calling to them.

Lucy and Fupi came at the back.

The animals sniffed the bushes and the grass, and some of them started to nibble. The zebra and the bushbuck, in particular, were happy to move away from Joel and were finding plenty to eat – they would soon be ready to be released. One of the baby warthogs grunted and made a run at Caspar, but he just jumped out of the way and they began a game of tag. Lucy had to grab Fupi's collar to stop her joining in.

Everywhere was so green and bright after the rain: the trees were coming into leaf, new grass was growing, and there was the wonderful smell of a previously parched landscape being revived. This was a country where the seasons were governed not by temperature or daylight length (which varied by hardly more than half an hour throughout the year) but by rainfall, with the long rains in March and April, and the short rains in September – except this year, when the short rains had forgotten to stop.

Lucy breathed in the wonderful fresh air and watched the orphan animals getting used to their freedom and their natural environment. She sat down with her back against a termite mound and noted what each animal ate and how it interacted with the others – things that would be important for when she became a wildlife vet.

There was a large rocky outcrop nearby. Craig had told them it was called a kopje and had a resident leopard. 'We'll keep well away from that naughty old leopard,' she said, as Caspar trotted up and sniffed her hand. He waggled his tail as if he understood then ran off doing little skips and jumps, before settling down to nibble some more leaves.

'I don't want you to…'

A brown blur erupted from some bushes and sped straight at Caspar.

'No!' screamed Lucy, leaping to her feet.

Joel shouted.

The jackal took no notice.

Caspar looked up just in time, twisted to the side and fled, the jackal snapping at his heels.

The little dik-dik twisted and turned, but the jackal followed every move and seemed to be gaining.

Joel hurled a stone. It hit the jackal on the flank. The animal yelped but was put off for only a second.

Lucy and Joel joined the chase but they had no hope of rescuing Caspar.

Suddenly, another blur joined in, but this one was brown and white.

The jackal didn't see Fupi until it was too late. It rolled over as Fupi crashed into it. Then it picked itself up from the dust, whirled round and fled, its tail between its legs and Fupi still in pursuit.

'Caspar!' cried Lucy. 'Are you all right?'

The little antelope looked up and trotted over to her. She scooped him into her arms and hugged him. She could feel his heart pounding and his body trembling. 'Oh, Caspar, I'm so glad that horrid jackal didn't get you.'

Fupi returned, wagging her tail and panting furiously.

'Fupi, you were brilliant!' cried Lucy, handing Caspar to Joel and picking up the little dog.

'That one is very fierce – *kali sana*,' said Joel, smiling and tickling Fupi's ears.

Lucy was sure that Fupi was grinning as she wagged her tail even faster.

∞◑◐∞

When they got back to the pens, Diana and Matata were feeding the other orphans, and Martha was waiting with Fupi's food bowl.

'Can I give it to her, Martha?' asked Lucy, as Fupi raced forward and bounced up and down trying to reach the bowl.

'There you are,' said Martha.

'Fupi, you've got to learn some manners,' said Lucy, taking the bowl. 'You must be patient. Sit.'

Fupi sat, her eyes riveted to the bowl.

'Stay,' said Lucy sternly, as Fupi was about to leap in. 'Stay,' she repeated, setting the bowl on the ground.

Fupi trembled with anticipation, not taking her eyes off her dinner.

'Go!'

Fupi leapt forward and began wolfing down the food.

'Not so fast, Fupi,' cried Lucy. 'You'll get indigestion.'

Fupi wagged her tail but wolfed even faster. She finished in no time and gave a hiccup and a loud burp.

'Serves you right, old greedy guts,' said Lucy, but secretly she was really relieved that Fupi hadn't lost her appetite after all the excitement. She watched the other animals finishing their respective feeds and then helped Matata collect and wash the empty bowls.

Kal wandered up bouncing a football on his feet. He wasn't interested in the animals but was waiting for Matata to finish so that they could continue their game.

'How's it going?' he asked.

'Kal, I need to think of a name for the new baby dik-dik,' said Lucy.

'Doris.'

'Doris! That's an awful name.'

'It begins with D.'

'So what?'

'All right, Doreen, then.'

'That's just as bad. Kal, you're hopeless.'

'Huh. I thought you wanted some help.'

'Yes, but not with stupid names like you might give an old granny.'

'I hope you weren't thinking of Diana,' said Diana, an amused smile on her face.

'That's even w...!' Lucy stopped and turned bright red.

Diana raised her eyebrows and smiled. 'Even what, Lucy?'

'Nothing,' said Lucy, and grinned. 'Anyway, I think it should begin with C, so that it goes with Caspar.'

'Custard,' said Kal.

'That's ridiculous. You're just saying the first thing that comes into your head.'

'Custard goes with Caspar – Caspar and Custard.'

'Oh do shut up,' said Lucy. 'Can you help, Diana?'

'I was wondering about Carnation,' said Diana. 'It's such a lovely flower.'

'Hmm,' said Lucy. That's also pretty crumby, she thought, but she didn't want to hurt Diana's feelings. 'I know,' she cried, 'Carmen – Caspar and Carmen!'

'Carmeni,' said Joel, who had been listening. '*Nzuri sana* – very good.'

'No, Carmen,' said Lucy.

'Yes,' said Joel, 'Carmeni.'

'No… Oh, never mind.'

'Car men!' cried Kal. 'What sort of a name is that?'

'Don't be thick,' said Lucy. 'Carmen is Spanish.'

'Right – just the name for a Tanzanian dik-dik, then.'

'You wouldn't understand.'

'I think Carmen is a very good name,' said Diana. 'I love the opera of that name.'

'*Ole!*' cried Kal, dancing round and clicking his fingers. 'Carmen, the singing dik-dik.'

'I'm not taking any notice of you,' said Lucy. 'It's Carmen, so there.'

Martha handed a food bowl to Lucy. 'That is for the new baby,' she said, 'for Carmeni.'

'For Carm…' Lucy sighed. 'Thanks, Martha,' she said, wondering whether Carmen was such a good name after all. But she wasn't going to change it. She carried the bowl to the back of the pen and set it down. 'Here, Carmen,' she called. The little animal stretched its head forward and sniffed at the bowl. 'Come on,' urged Lucy, keeping very still. The dik-dik looked at her and wiggled its nose, then got up, stretched itself and started to feed. Lucy noticed how thin it was. 'Good girl,' she murmured.

'That is very good, Lucy,' said Martha, 'soon that one will be better. Then who knows?' She gave a shrug. 'Perhaps there will be a marriage.'

Lucy passed the empty bowl to Martha. 'It would be so lovely if...'

'Hey, look, over there,' cried Kal, who had been leaning over the gate of the pen looking bored. 'It's a Cessna just like Craig's.' He pointed at a small plane flying along the edge of a nearby hillside. It turned towards them and swooped low over the house with a roar from the engine. Fupi barked.

'Who is it?' cried Lucy.

'I've no idea,' said Diana.

They watched the plane bank round.

'I think he's going to land,' cried Kal. 'I'll tell Craig.' He raced off.

CHAPTER 4

Warthog

THE RHINO

Kal and Craig sat in the open Land Rover at the end of the airstrip watching as the plane lined up to land. A family of warthogs was rooting in the grass at the side of the strip not in the least troubled by the plane's approach.

'Do you know who it is?' asked Kal.

'I'm not sure, but I think it could be The Rhino.'

'The Rhino!'

'That's it,' said Craig, smiling.

'That'll be a first, then,' said Kal, with a grin, 'a rhino flying a plane!'

Craig chuckled. 'He used to be the head of Tanzania's Game Parks, great friend of my dad's. His job took him all over the country, flying to visit the parks that were in his charge.'

'And that was work?'

Craig nodded. 'Some job, hey? To start with, he had to drive everywhere, but then an American team came to make a film about wildlife in the parks. They didn't have much time so they bought a plane to travel quickly, then gave it to him when they'd finished.'

'They gave him a plane!'

'And paid for his flying lessons. They said the time they saved more than paid for the costs.'

'Wish I could get a job like that,' said Kal with feeling. 'But why's he called rhino?'

'His real name is George Kafaro, but the newspapers changed it to Kifaru (Faru for short), which means rhino in Swahili. That was after he bullied the government into giving park rangers proper salaries and decent vehicles. The press loved his style: charge in and ask questions afterwards, just like the rhino. He did a great job in Parks and helped a lot to cut down poaching.'

'What do you call him?'

'I call him Faru – like everyone else. The name has stuck.'

Kal heard the pilot throttle back the engine. 'Any idea why he's visiting now?' he asked.

'No, I... Look out!' yelled Craig. He leapt out of the Land Rover and ran towards the plane, waving his arms. One of the warthogs – a big solid male – had wandered onto the airstrip.

Kal raced after Craig.

The warthog looked up – but not at the plane. It was staring straight at *them* wondering what all the fuss was about.

'The pilot hasn't seen it,' cried Kal with a sense of terrible foreboding.

The two of them shouted louder and waved more frantically.

The warthog cocked its head and stayed looking at them, not moving.

Kal saw the nose of the plane come up as the pilot prepared to land. If he hadn't seen the warthog earlier, he couldn't possibly see it now with his view obscured.

Kal and Craig watched, frozen, helpless, as the plane's wheels touched down. A short bounce, then it was speeding over the ground.

The warthog spun round and saw the plane – too late.

'No!' yelled Kal.

One of the wheels struck the warthog throwing it aside. The plane slewed round, came to a shuddering halt and tipped onto its nose. The propeller snapped. There was a brief roar from the engine before it stalled.

The warthog lay still for a moment, then picked itself up, raced over to its companions and all of them fled into the bush.

There was no movement from the plane.

'Quick!' yelled Craig. He and Kal raced back to the Land Rover, jumped in and tore down the strip to the stricken plane.

'We daren't go too close, in case she goes up,' cried Craig, slamming on the brakes. 'Stay here,' he ordered, as he leapt out.

Kal ignored him.

'Stay away!' shouted Craig, turning to Kal and waving him back. As he turned, he tripped and fell heavily to the ground.

Kal was past him and racing to the plane, Craig's words: "*in case she goes up*", ringing in his ears.

He reached the plane.

A large man was slumped over the controls. Was he alive? Was he dead? Kal had no way of knowing. Finding out could wait. What terrified him was the smell, the smell of fuel – highly inflammable fuel leaking onto a hot engine. "*In case she goes up*". Kal tore at the door of the plane. It was jammed. He kicked it. Nothing. Still that awful smell.

Craig arrived, wrenched at the door and almost tore it off its hinges.

The man didn't move. Craig pushed him aside and groped under the instrument panel to close off the fuel supply. He then stood back and wiped a hand across his face. 'That could have been very nasty,' he said, 'for all of us.'

Kal nodded. Suddenly his legs felt very weak and he had to grab hold of the wing to steady himself. 'Is... is he okay?' he stammered.

Craig gently shook the man's shoulder. He gave a groan.

'He's alive, thank goodness,' muttered Craig. 'But no way of knowing how badly he's hurt.'

'Is he the one we were talking about?' asked Kal.

'Faru. Yes, poor guy.' Craig reached into the cramped space of the cockpit and released the man's seat belt. 'Faru, are you okay? It's me, Craig.'

The man made no response.

'Can you hear me?'

Still no response.

'Come on, let's get you out of there.' Craig tried to lift him clear.

The man slumped sideways, but seemed to be wedged into the tight space.

Craig tried again, struggling within the confines of the cramped cockpit.

The man gave another groan.

'Can I help?' asked Kal.

Craig shook his head. 'Not enough space,' he panted, sweat soaking through his shirt with the effort. 'He's a big guy and I can't get enough leverage.'

He tried once more. 'It's no good,' he said. 'Kal, I'll stay here with him, you go and find Samson and tell him to bring hacksaws and bolt-cutters, anything we might need to cut this thing open. And bring my first-aid case,' he added.

Kal nodded and was gone.

Kal had never driven faster in the Land Rover. Mum would have been horrified if she'd seen the speedometer. Kal wasn't even aware, his thoughts were focused on getting to the house as quickly as possible, finding Samson, finding tools and the first-aid case, and getting back before some fuel found its way onto a hot exhaust pipe.

Kal pressed his foot harder to the floor. He reached the end of the airstrip and had to slacken speed as he weaved along the muddy track through the trees. Some baboons were ambling along ahead of him. Kal hit the horn and they scattered right and left, fleeing with screams of outrage. Foot to the floor again. The Land Rover slewed sideways. Kal corrected the skid, and two giraffes feeding on the topmost branches of a tree, lumbered off in startled alarm. Some vervet monkeys shouted abuse from another tree.

Kal was barely aware. His hand was still on the horn as he reached the house. Everyone had run out to see the cause of the commotion.

Kal skidded to a halt. 'It's the Rhino. He's hit a warthog,' he yelled, leaping out and leaving the engine running.

'The rhino hit a warthog?' cried Lucy. 'What are you talking about?'

'Fa… Fa something. Big guy.'

'Faru?' cried Diana.

'That's it. He's crashed.'

'Oh my Lord!' Diana's hand flew to her mouth. 'Is he…?'

'Where's Samson?'

'Here,' yelled a voice, as Samson and Matata came running round the side of the house. 'What is it?'

'The plane crashed and the guy's stuck inside,' cried Kal. 'We need tools and things to cut him out.'

'Right. Matata, come!' shouted Samson, beckoning to his son. The two of them raced off.

'Is he… is he…?' Diana's voice was fraught.

'He seems okay,' said Kal, 'but Craig can't shift him. We're really worried in case…'

'In case what?' cried Lucy, who was clutching Fupi in her arms.

'Nothing,' said Kal. 'Diana, where's Craig's first-aid case?'

'It should be in the office, but are you sure Faru's…?'

Kal pushed past her, bounded up the steps of the veranda, flung open the office door, grabbed the case from under a table, and tore back to the Land Rover. He reached it just as Samson and Matata arrived breathless and sweating, clutching armfuls of tools, which they flung into the back.

'We may need the other Landy,' shouted Samson. 'I'll bring that. You and Matata go ahead with the tools.'

Matata jumped in beside Kal, and they sped back to the plane.

⌘

Kal was terrified what they might see when they reached the airstrip: columns of black smoke, a blazing inferno, charred remains.

They came clear of the trees. Kal peered through the mud-spattered windscreen. The plane was as he'd left it, tilted on its nose, and Craig was standing beside it waving.

Matata waved back.

'Thank goodness,' muttered Kal. He put his foot to the floor and tore down the airstrip, bringing the Land Rover skidding to a halt a safe distance from the plane.

'Well done, guys,' shouted Craig.

The two boys raced across to him.

36

'Where's Samson?'

'*Nakuja* – he comes,' cried Matata, pointing to where Samson's Land Rover had just emerged from the trees.

'How's Faru?' asked Kal.

'Not much change, but he's moaning a bit more. That was a lucky escape.'

'The plane looks a bit of a mess.'

'Could have been a lot worse, though. As far as I can tell, the only serious damage is the broken prop.'

'Will you be able to fix it?'

Before Craig could respond, Samson arrived and joined them. He grimaced as he surveyed the plane. 'It looks bad,' he said.

'I can't shift him,' said Craig. 'I guess we'll have to cut him out. You've brought the tools?'

Samson nodded then peered into the cramped space of the cockpit. 'He doesn't appear to be trapped and... let's see.' He wrapped his powerful arms round Faru's chest. '*Bwana*, I'm going to try and move you,' he said in a loud voice. 'Matata, *shika mlango* – hold the door.'

Matata held the door as far back as he could. Samson bent his knees, the muscles on his arms bulged and knotted as he leaned back and began to straighten his legs. He grunted with the strain and his shirt split open. The veins stood out on his neck and sweat poured off his face, but Faru was coming free.

Samson gritted his teeth and heaved, and Faru's body came free of the cockpit. Craig squeezed past and helped lift his legs clear.

They carried Faru away from the plane and laid him on the ground. Craig began to check him over.

'Nasty bang on the forehead but no broken bones as far as I can tell,' he said. 'He's a good colour, so no serious bleeding.' He looked up and grinned at Kal. 'Now you know how Samson got his name.'

'That was awesome,' murmured Kal.

Samson shrugged and wiped his brow with his torn shirt.

Matata flexed his own biceps and they all laughed.

Faru started to cough. Craig sat him up and the coughing subsided.

'You're okay, Faru,' he shouted. 'You had a bit of a spill.'

Faru opened his eyes. 'Wh... what?'

'It's me, Craig.'

'Craig?' Faru's voice was shaky and he seemed to have trouble focusing. 'That you?'

'Yes, we'll soon have you on your feet again.'

Faru made as though to stand up.

'Whoa there,' cried Craig.

Faru slumped back to the ground.

'I'll get my Landy,' said Samson, and ran back to his vehicle.

They laid Faru on the floor in the back and tried to make him comfortable by bunching an old tarpaulin under his head. Craig and Matata climbed in beside him.

'Kal, you follow,' called Craig. 'We'll sort the plane out later. Okay, Samson, *tuende* – let's go. Take it slowly.'

Kal was just about to drive off in the other Land Rover when his eye caught a movement away to his left. A family of warthogs was watching him – a large male standing in front. Kal slowly shook his head, had a last look at the upended plane then followed after the others.

CHAPTER 5

Red-chested cuckoo

AN EXCITING PLAN

Lucy held a basin of warm water, while Diana sponged the blood off Faru's forehead. Ellie stood ready with swabs and bandages. Kal and Craig watched.

'You've had a nasty bang there,' said Diana.

'Had worse,' muttered Faru. He had now fully recovered consciousness, and apart from a large lump above his right eye, seemed none the worse for his ordeal.

Lucy studied him as he lay on the sofa clearly enjoying all the attention. He was a large elderly man with startlingly white hair against his dark skin. He wore baggy jeans, a faded blue shirt and safari boots without socks. He reminded her of a famous South African politician but she couldn't remember his name.

'Sorry to arrive out of the blue like this,' Faru said, still with his eyes closed, 'but I was just passing so I thought I'd drop in.'

Just passing, thought Lucy. Simba's in the middle of nowhere, but I suppose if you've got your own plane, you can just *drop in*.

'You certainly arrived in style,' said Craig.

Faru grunted. 'What happened?'

'You hit a warthog.'

'Never saw a thing.'

'You were very lucky.'

'Now, keep still,' commanded Diana, 'while we get you bandaged up.'

'Lot of fuss over a little scratch,' muttered Faru, but made no move to resist.

Diana swathed his head in a large bandage and secured it at the back of his head. 'There you are, good as new.'

Faru continued to mutter.

'Can I ask what really brought you this way, Faru?' asked Craig.

'No, you may not,' said Diana, before Faru could reply. 'Faru needs to rest. We'll set up a mosquito net over the sofa after supper, and he can spend the night here.'

Faru made a gesture of helplessness.

'Off you go, all of you,' said Diana, 'and let Faru have some peace.' She shooed them off the veranda.

Next morning, Faru joined them for breakfast. His bandage was still in place but the accident didn't seem to have spoiled his appetite.

'Very good of you to put me up,' he said, as he tucked into bacon and eggs.

'Not at all, it was the least we could do,' said Diana.

'How are you feeling?' asked Ellie.

'Bit sore and a few bruises, otherwise not too bad.'

'You must stay here and take things easy for a few days,' said Diana.

'Well, I...'

'I insist. Anyway, your plane's in a mess so you can't possibly leave until it's fixed. I can't believe we've now got two damaged planes,' she muttered, pouring more tea for Faru.

'Two?' he queried.

Craig explained.

'Hmm, bad business, doesn't bear thinking about.'

'Bad things always happen in threes,' observed Lucy.

'Great,' said Kal. 'That's really made my day.'

'I was only saying.'

'Don't.'

'But it's true. You just see.'

'Well paint me purple and throw me to the lions,' muttered Kal.

'You what?' said Lucy.

'You heard,' said Kal. 'Let's get it over with, so we can get on with our lives.'

'Hey, you guys,' said Craig, 'let's talk about something a bit more cheerful.'

'Silly superstition,' said Diana. 'I've no time for such nonsense.'

'Quite right,' said Faru. He had a deep rich voice that reminded Lucy of distant thunder or surf rumbling on a beach – or was it thick chocolate?

'Moving on,' said Craig, 'the good news, Faru, is that apart from the broken prop, your plane seems okay. Kal and I checked it out. We reckon we could fit the propeller from my plane onto yours then we'd at least have one that was serviceable.'

Faru shook his head. 'Couldn't possibly leave you here without wings.'

Craig smiled. 'Let me tell you the rest of the plan, then. Since Mother is insisting – and rightly so – that you stay here for a few days, perhaps I could borrow your plane after we've fixed it, fly up to Nairobi and collect the spares for mine. I can't get them locally and it would save me a long drive.'

'Excellent plan, provided you good people can put up with me here,' said Faru.

'Faru, you are most welcome,' said Diana. 'It's ages since we've seen you and I look forward to hearing all your news.'

Faru smiled and gave a gesture of helplessness.

Craig set his coffee mug down and rested his elbows on the table. 'Now, Faru, you really do have to tell us why you decided to pay us a visit.'

'As I said, just passing.'

Craig shook his head. 'Faru, I know you too well to believe that.'

Faru gave a mock sigh. 'All right,' he said, giving his rumbling chuckle. 'I'd been visiting my son Nathan – he's the warden of the Serengeti National Park,' he added for the benefit of the children. 'I asked him if he could take some of my roans.'

'Your roans?' exclaimed Craig.

Faru nodded. 'Herd's getting too big and I need to reduce it. Couldn't possibly think of culling them.'

'No way,' agreed Craig. 'What was Nathan's answer?'

'He wasn't keen. Too much paperwork, he said.'

Craig laughed. 'You were the one who made those rules, Faru.'

Faru smiled ruefully. 'I know. Now I'm the one who's been caught out by them.'

Lucy's eyes darted between the two men. What were they talking about, and what were roans?

'So what now?' asked Craig.

Faru gave Craig a quizzical look. 'Nathan suggested you might be able to help.'

'Me? How?'

Lucy couldn't contain herself any longer. 'What are roans?' she blurted.

'They're a kind of antelope, Lucy,' said Craig, 'rather like a small pony.'

'Are they rare?'

'They're rare in this part of Tanzania, but not further south.'

'And you've got some, Mister Faru?' said Lucy.

'Lucy,' said Faru, his eyes twinkling, 'I would far rather you call me Faru, like everyone else – much less formal. But if you insist, you can call me *Bwana* Faru, but not mister. You are in Africa.'

Lucy thought for a moment. 'Okay,' she said. 'I'll call you Faru; it's the sort of name that makes me think of adventures.'

Faru gave his rich chuckle. 'You like adventures, do you?'

Lucy nodded.

'Well, well. But to answer your question, Lucy: I do have some roans – too many now for the reserve, in fact.'

'You live on a reserve?' cried Lucy. 'A real wildlife reserve?'

'I do indeed – a combined coastal and marine reserve. When I retired from my post as head of parks, my successor asked me if I would look after a small reserve down at the coast. My wife had recently died and he suggested it would help take my mind off things.'

'We were very sorry to hear the news, Faru,' said Diana.

Faru nodded. 'The reserve was just the distraction I needed,' he said. 'I don't have too much to do. The place mostly looks after itself.'

'I'm sure that's not true,' said Craig, smiling. 'I bet you're out there all the time.'

Faru shrugged. 'Well, I like to make sure the local people don't damage the marine environment, illegal fishing and shell collecting, for instance, nor poach the animals, start fires and cut down the trees – that sort of thing.'

'What animals have you got there?' asked Lucy.

'Mostly the roans, and what lives in the local forest. There are some rare birds and, of course, elephant-shrews. That's how we persuaded Government to designate the area as a reserve.'

'Elephant what?'

'It's a wind-up,' said Kal.

'Not at all,' said Faru, his eyes twinkling. 'They're reddish brown fellows with yellow backsides, about the size of the little dog there.' He indicated Fupi.

Lucy frowned. She didn't think Fupi looked at all like a shrew.

'Coming back to the roans,' said Craig, 'what exactly did Nathan suggest?'

'He wondered if you could perhaps er... take some here.'

'It would be lovely to have some roans,' said Diana, 'they're so beautiful.'

'Yes,' murmured Craig, stroking his chin. 'Also pretty *kali* – pretty fierce, and they can be dangerous.'

'Most of mine are now used to people,' said Faru. 'There shouldn't be a problem.'

Craig gazed out across the lawn. 'I suppose we could put them near the Seki Hills – habitat there would be all right.' He indicated the hills in the distance.

'Have you still got that truck you use for translocation?' asked Faru.

Craig nodded.

Lucy had seen programmes on television about capturing wild animals and moving them to other places where they would be safer or where there was more space for them. Now, here was Craig being asked if he could translocate some rare antelopes to Simba. She couldn't believe it. 'I'll help,' she blurted.

'Splendid!' cried Faru. 'Can you ride?'

'Er... yes. We sometimes go riding in Richmond Park – there's loads of deer there. Ellie can as well.'

'Lucy!' cried Ellie. 'What are you saying?'

'I'm saying we know how to ride.'

'Yes, but… Faru, why do you want to know if we can ride?'

'To help round up the roans, my dear; they're not afraid of horses.'

'I see.' Ellie wasn't reassured.

'What about you, young Kal, do you ride?' asked Faru.

'No way! I don't do livestock.'

'You'd better use the quad bike, then.'

Kal grinned. 'Wicked!'

'Won't that be brilliant!' cried Lucy. 'We'll all be able to help.'

Craig held up his hands. 'Before you guys get too carried away, you may not have noticed, but it's actually rather wet.'

'It's not raining,' said Kal.

'Not at the moment, but we need at least two dry days before we could think of getting the truck off. Then there are other things we have to think about.'

'Like what?' said Lucy.

'Your parents arriving shortly.'

'Oh, that,' said Lucy.

Craig raised his eyebrows and smiled. 'Yes – that.'

'Dad's a professor at the university in Nairobi,' said Lucy.

'Is that so?' said Faru.

'Yes, he's…'

'And we have a plane – two planes – to repair,' continued Craig. 'But getting them sorted isn't going to help us with the roans. If this weather continues, things won't happen until after Christmas and you kids have gone back to school.'

Lucy looked at the grey overcast sky. 'Isn't that just typical!'

'Talking of Christmas,' said Diana, 'what are you doing, Faru, over the holiday?'

'Me?' Faru smiled. 'I'm too old for Christmas.'

'You're not old,' cried Lucy.

'Thank you, my dear,' said Faru with a chuckle.

'Let me make a suggestion,' said Diana. 'Why don't you stay here for Christmas? It will mean staying only a few extra days, and you will be near Nathan and his family so you can see them as well.'

'Thank you, Diana,' said Faru. 'That is most kind, but I do need to get back to the reserve. I have a couple of fellows helping out but I don't like leaving them on their own for too long.'

'I'm sure they'll be fine,' said Craig.

Faru shook his head. 'No, I can't risk things slipping.' He paused. 'But let me make an alternative suggestion.' He looked round the gathering and beamed. 'Why don't you come to me at the coast – all of you? How's that? If the rain stops, that is.'

'Faru, we couldn't possibly impose, there's far too many of us,' cried Diana.

'Nonsense. I'm on my own now so there's plenty of room. Some of you might have to sleep outside on the veranda, though.'

'Cool,' said Kal.

'Actually,' said Faru, 'it will probably be rather hot.'

'Where exactly *do* you live, Faru?' asked Lucy.

'Place called Watumwani, overlooks the sea – not a bad place.'

'Watumwani?' said Ellie, frowning. 'I've read that name somewhere. Hold on.' She hurried off to the sitting room and came back carrying an atlas of Tanzania, which she opened on the floor. 'I borrowed some of your books, Craig, to read up about the... Here!' She pointed to a dot on the map. 'It's one of the places where the Arab slave-traders used to go.'

'That's right,' said Faru. 'There are supposed to be some old Arab ruins on the reserve.'

'Supposed to be?' said Lucy. 'Don't you know?'

'If they exist they'll be somewhere in the forest, but it's all overgrown. There's even talk of a cave where slaves were kept but I've never found it.'

46

'A cave!' cried Lucy. 'Ellie, show Faru the message we found in our cave.'

'What message? What cave?' asked Faru.

'When we crashed,' said Lucy. 'We found something scratched on the wall of the cave where we had to spend the night. Ellie says it's writing.'

'Here we are,' said Ellie. She drew out the slip of paper that was tucked in the front of the atlas and passed it to Faru.

He rummaged in his shirt pocket for his glasses. 'Right, what have we got here?' He peered at the paper. 'Hmm, it's certainly writing – probably Arabic – but I've no idea what it means.'

'Do you know anyone who could translate it?' asked Ellie.

'Abdul Raman would be the person. He's the curator of archaeology at the museum in Dar es Salaam.'

'Could we take it and show him when we come to the coast?'

'Yes, of course.'

Lucy's eyes were shining. 'I can't wait to get...'

'Hear that?' said Craig, indicating a tree on the far side of the lawn.

They could all hear the clear three-note call: "*wip wip weeoo*".

'What is it?' said Lucy.

'That's the rain bird – the red-chested cuckoo – it's supposed to be saying: "*it will rain*". It's usually right.'

There was a great thunderclap and large drops of rain started to fall.

'No-o-o!' wailed Lucy.

CHAPTER 6

Klipspringer

EAGLES DON'T LIKE DOGS

Two days later, Craig and Kal returned from Nairobi in Faru's plane, which appeared none the worse for its crash. Samson drove down to the airstrip to collect them, and when they got back to the house, Dad was with them.

'Surprise,' he said, as he hugged the girls in turn. 'Craig phoned to say there was a spare seat in the plane, so I thought I'd come down early.'

'That's great, Dad,' said Lucy.

'I can't wait to get back to the Seki Hills,' enthused Dad. 'The recent precipitation will undoubtedly have exposed new strata, which could be quite informative.'

'What does that mean?' asked Lucy.

'Dad means that it's been raining and some new rocks might have been uncovered,' said Ellie.

Dad frowned and turned to Craig. 'When do you think we'll be able to get up to there?'

Craig stroked his chin. 'It shouldn't take too long to fix my plane now we've got the spares. The weather seems to be clearing up, so if it holds we should be able to go…'

'Tomorrow?' cried Lucy.

'Fingers crossed.'

Next morning the weather was even brighter, Craig's plane had been repaired, and now Craig, Kal, Lucy and Dad were on their way to the Seki Hills. And perhaps, just perhaps, they *would* get to the coast.

'Fupi, that would just be so brilliant,' Lucy whispered to the little dog sitting on her lap.

The two of them peered at the fresh green landscape below. The view was so clear now that the rain had washed the dust out of the air, and Lucy could see the summit of Mount Kilimanjaro startlingly bright in the distance.

Craig landed on the bumpy airstrip they had prepared on their previous visit, and Lucy was relieved there were no ominous sounds from the undercarriage. Craig stopped the engine and they climbed out to find Joel and Matata waiting for them.

'What are you doing here?' cried Lucy.

'We are *askaris*,' said Matata, proudly brandishing his spear. 'We come to guard rocks.'

Craig smiled. 'I've organised a roster,' he said, 'two guys up here for a week at a time. We don't want any more trouble with outsiders trying to steal the rubies.'

'Where do you stay, Joel?' asked Lucy.

'*Huko* – up there.' Joel pointed to a massive cliff face that ran along the foot of the hills in front of them. 'We will take you.'

'Any news, Joel?' asked Craig.

'The news is good,' said Joel, emptying the contents of a plastic bag onto the ground. 'We found these stones.'

'Good Lord!' exclaimed Dad, kneeling down and examining them.

'Are they rubies, Dad?' asked Lucy.

'Yes, yes. They most certainly are. Superb – absolutely superb.' Dad held one of the stones up to the light. It was mostly dark green but there was a large piece embedded in it that was glinting bluish-red. 'Wonderful, wonderful.' He pulled a hand lens out of his pocket and began humming tunelessly to himself as he examined each stone in turn.

'Did they come from the Place of the Skull, where we found the stones last time?' asked Lucy.

'No, that is more far that way,' said Joel, pointing.

'Off we go, then.' Dad set off.

'David,' called Craig. 'Be a good idea to have a snack. At least, have a drink.'

'Yes, of course,' said Dad, returning. 'Sorry, getting carried away, but I must say, this is all most exciting.'

They settled in the shade of the wing and shared their lunch with Joel and Matata.

'Has the site been gazetted yet?' asked Dad, as he munched his sandwich.

'Don't talk with your mouth full,' murmured Lucy.

Kal sniggered.

'The paperwork is almost complete,' said Craig, 'then we'll carry out a proper survey before we begin controlled mining operations.'

'I'd be pleased to supervise that,' said Dad. 'You'd probably appreciate someone with my experience.'

'Can you spare the time?'

Dad waved a dismissive hand. 'Delighted, delighted.' He shaded his eyes and gazed at the hillside that rose up behind them. 'Fascinating spot, this – absolutely fascinating.'

'It will be such a shame to spoil it,' said Lucy.

'That won't happen,' said Craig. ' I want to keep the operation low key, partly so we don't get nosey people taking an interest but mainly so that we don't spoil a beautiful place.'

'Environmental considerations are most important,' said Dad, 'I'll ensure that the disturbance is minimal. The fact that inexperienced people are finding material of this quality, suggests that the deposits are close to the surface and can be easily reached.'

'It will be good for the ranch, won't it,' said Lucy, 'having the extra money?'

'Government will take quite a bit,' said Craig, 'but there should be plenty for everyone, and for other developments.'

'Other developments?' said Lucy.

'A school. There are no schools near here, so most of the kids do their schooling in the bush.'

'That would suit me,' said Kal.

'Me too,' said Lucy.

Craig smiled.

'When will you start?' asked Kal.

'As soon as we get the clearance. The Minister of Environment and Conservation, who's on the board, is pushing things through. He's very supportive of the school idea and has also suggested we build a small lodge for eco-tourism.'

'What, and charge rich Americans and Japanese oodles to stay in it?' said Lucy.

'Not quite.' Craig laughed. 'I was thinking of something a little less up-market: walking safaris – that sort of thing – something to appeal to people who want to get close to Africa.'

'I'll help supervise that,' said Lucy, grinning. 'You'd probably appreciate someone with my experience.'

Craig winked at her. 'Can you spare the time?'

'I'll tell my secretary to keep you informed of my availability, but I…'

'*Ona* – see,' cried Matata, pointing at a large bird that had sailed into view.

'Bateleur!' cried Lucy. 'Fantastic!'

'Battle-axe?' said Kal.

'No, you idiot! A bateleur – it's a kind of eagle.'

'Why's it flying backwards?'

'Don't be daft – it's got a short tail. Look, there's another.'

Fupi tilted her head and watched as the two birds glided effortlessly along in the updraft from the cliff.

One of the birds suddenly seemed to fall out of the sky, tumbling over in the air.

'It's been shot!' cried Lucy.

The other bird followed it, and both rolled over.

'They're fine. It's their courtship display,' said Craig. 'See.' The birds righted themselves and resumed their effortless flight along the cliff face.

'They are making a house there,' said Joel, 'in that tree.'

Lucy looked through her binoculars at a big tree growing out of the cliff, but couldn't see the nest.

'That's where we're going,' said Craig. 'We may get a better view from above. Let's go.' He closed up the plane, hitched the rucksack onto his back, and they set off.

Matata led them round the end of the cliff and then up a steep game trail. They struggled on for over an hour and still hadn't reached the top.

'Is it much further?' panted Lucy, 'I'm...'

Her words were cut short by a rattle of stones from above. Matata pointed. Two animals with large round ears peered down at them from the edge of a cliff-face.

'They're going to fall!' cried Lucy.

'Not these guys,' said Craig.

'Are they goats?' asked Kal.

'*Mbuzi ya mawe* – goats of the rocks,' said Joel.

'That's their Swahili name,' said Craig. 'We call them klipspringers, a sort of rock antelope.'

'It looks really dangerous up there,' said Lucy, as she studied them through her binoculars.

'I wouldn't want to be up there,' agreed Craig, 'but their feet are specially adapted to grip the rocks.'

The klipspringers, which had been watching them, gave a snort and went racing away across the precipitous slope.

'Awesome,' murmured Kal.

They struggled on up the game trail. Finally, it began to level off and they could see a series of smaller cliffs beyond them.

'Phew,' said Dad, 'that was quite a climb.'

'Have we got to go up there as well?' asked Lucy, slumping to the ground.

'A short way,' said Joel. 'There is something you must see in the place where we stay.'

'What?'

'Have a drink first,' said Craig, passing round a water bottle.

Some hyraxes, which reminded Lucy of large guinea pigs, were sitting on nearby rocks eyeing them suspiciously.

A shadow flitted over the sun. The hyraxes squeaked in alarm and dived into crevices. The bateleurs sailed overhead. Now they were closer, Lucy could see their black and grey plumage, and even the bright red around their beaks.

'They're beautiful,' she murmured. 'Do they go for hyraxes?'

'They will,' said Craig, 'even animals as large as dik-diks, but mostly birds and lizards – like that agama.' He pointed at a large lizard with a bright blue head, which was watching them from a nearby rock.

'I think we should be moving on,' said Dad. 'Is it much further?'

'Very near,' said Joel. 'Come.'

They followed him for another few hundred metres and came to an area where the recent rain had cut deep gullies in the soft ground.

'Ah!' exclaimed Dad, and scrambled down into one of the gullies. He immediately started tapping around with a geological hammer. 'What have we here?' He extracted a small rock and peered at it through a hand lens. 'Hmm, promising, promising.' He slipped the rock into a bag he had strapped to his waist then continued his search, his recent tiredness forgotten.

'David, could we leave you here with Joel,' called Craig, 'while we go off and see if we can find the bateleur's nest?'

'What was that?' said Dad, looking up.

'Will you be all right, if we leave you with Joel?'

'Yes, yes.' Dad waved. 'Bye. Ah ha, what's this?'

'I guess Dad's happy,' said Kal.

Craig grinned. 'Okay, Matata, what is it you want to show us?'

'Come.'

Matata led them up the hillside to one of the smaller cliffs. There was an overhang at one point where a creeper, trailing down from above, partly hid a recess in the rock face. Two blankets were draped over bushes outside.

'*Nyumba yetu* – our house,' said Matata.

'Is this where you stay?' asked Lucy.

Matata nodded.

'It looks jolly cosy. And is that where you cook?' She pointed to the remains of a fire with three large stones placed round it and a blackened cooking pot beside.

'It is kitchen,' he said, smiling. '*Kuja* – come.' He led them further along where the recess was deeper. He pulled the creepers aside to let the light in and pointed.

Lucy gasped. The scribbles on the wall looked exactly like those in the cave where they had slept the previous week. 'Are they the same, Craig?'

Craig examined the marks. 'I guess they could be, which means that…'

'The Arabs came through here as well,' cried Lucy.

'Could be.' Craig took the notebook from his shirt pocket and began copying down the symbols. 'We'll have to compare them when we get back.'

'What does it all mean?' said Lucy, a note of awe in her voice.

Matata led them back to the main cliff, and they stood above a point where it was almost sheer to the bottom far below. '*Ona* – see,' he said, pointing downwards.

They crept closer to the edge and peered over.

Lucy didn't dare go too close but she could just make out what looked like a large fig tree growing out of a crack in the rock face. She lay down on her stomach, wriggled forward and focused her binoculars on the tree. Fupi stood beside her trying to work out what was so interesting.

Craig and Kal were also lying and peering over the edge.

'I think I can see a nest,' said Lucy. 'It's…'

There was a rush of wings, a yelp from Fupi, and Lucy felt the draught of air as one of the bateleurs swooped over them.

She screamed.

Fupi was gone.

CHAPTER 7

Bateleur eagle

EAGLES DON'T LIKE PEOPLE

'Fupi!' screamed Lucy. She peered over the edge, leaning out as far as she dare.

There was no sign.

'The eagle's taken her!'

She wriggled back from the edge, buried her head in her hands and burst into tears. 'Fupi, oh Fupi!'

Craig knelt down and put an arm round her shoulder.

She turned and threw her arms round him and sobbed. 'Poor Fupi. It's all my fault. I should have been looking after her.'

'No, if it's anyone's fault, it's mine,' muttered Craig. 'I should have realised the birds would try and protect their nest.'

'What are we going to do?' Lucy was distraught.

There was a shout from Matata. '*Naweza kuona* – I can see!' he cried. He had moved along the cliff and was pointing over the edge.

Lucy raced across and might have gone straight over if he hadn't grabbed her.

'Where?' she cried.

'*Huko chini* – down there.'

Far beneath them on a narrow ledge below the fig tree, she could see a white speck. It wasn't moving.

Lucy focused her binoculars. It *was* Fupi. She was lying very still, and Lucy could see another colour on her back. Red!

'Oh no,' she wailed.

Craig lay down on the edge and looked through his own binoculars. 'How on earth do we get down there?' he muttered.

'I go,' said Matata. 'I go and see.' He ran along the edge of the cliff searching for a way down. '*Hapa*,' he called, and disappeared.

The others ran to the spot. Matata was creeping down a slight gully, using roots and projecting rocks as hand and footholds.

'Matata, *rudi* – come back!' yelled Craig. 'It's not safe.'

One of the bateleurs swooped over them again. They barely noticed.

The rock on which Matata was standing gave way and crashed off down the cliff. It bounced off a projecting rock and hit nothing until it reached the ground far below. Matata was now hanging by one hand from a tree root, kicking his legs and trying to find a foothold. His left foot located a rock. He eased his weight onto it. The rock came away and followed the other to the bottom.

The root that Matata was holding snapped.

He yelled.

There was nothing to stop his hurtling to the bottom – except the projecting rock some three metres below. He crashed into it. His scrabbling hands managed to grab hold of a bush. He was safe – for the moment. But he was ten metres below them. And there was no way back.

'*Shika sana* – hold on,' yelled Craig. 'We'll get you back.'

Matata looked up and grinned.

Lucy couldn't believe he was actually grinning!

'*Naendalea* – I go,' he called.

'He's crazy to carry on,' muttered Craig. 'Matata, *ngoja* – wait! Come back!'

Matata didn't appear to hear.

'I can't look,' whispered Lucy, her hands over her face.

'He's doing really well,' said Kal.

'Where is he?' Still, she daren't look.

'He's reached the tree with the nest in it.'

There was a screech overhead. One of the eagles swooped down and hurtled towards Matata.

'Look out!' yelled Kal.

Matata looked up, and managed to duck just as the eagle swept over him, its talons reaching for his head. '*Sawa tu* – I okay,' he shouted, as the bird sailed off. He continued downwards, now climbing more easily using the roots from the tree as handholds. Then he was there – there on the narrow ledge beside Fupi.

Lucy peered through her binoculars and could see Fupi's tail trying to wag.

'Fupi's alive!' she cried.

'Yes, but now what?' muttered Craig.

They held their breath as they watched Matata pick Fupi up and tuck her under one arm, then the other, then try different ways of holding her. But there was no way that he could climb back using only one hand.

'Now they're both stuck,' wailed Lucy.

'Kal,' said Craig, 'could you find your way back to the plane?'

'Sure.' Kal scrambled to his feet.

'There's a rope behind the rear seats. Could you…?'

Kal was gone before Craig could finish the sentence.

∽⤳⤳∾

Kal recalled the last time he had run in these hills, when that man who'd shot Craig had chased him. This time, he was in no danger of being shot but how long would it take to run back to the plane, and how long could Mat cling on with Fupi?

He tried to picture Reuben Kalima, the Olympic gold medallist after whom he had acquired his nickname of Kal, and whom they'd met on their last visit. Remember what Reuben had said about relaxing the shoulders, controlling the breathing, keeping the rhythm of his stride.

He passed the spot where they had left Dad and Joel. There was no sign of them. Kal missed the game trail that led down from the cliff and wasted precious minutes having to retrace his steps. Then he found it. He started off too fast, slipping and sliding on the loose stones.

Slow down. You can't afford to get injured.

He grabbed a tree, nearly wrenching his arms out of their sockets.

There was a snort, a rattle of stones, and Kal's heart flew into his mouth.

The klipspringers bounded away.

He continued more slowly but with no less urgency.

He reached the plane and checked his watch. It had taken him half an hour. He could never get back in that time.

He threw open the door of the plane and lay panting for a moment. Then he slid the front seat forward and climbed into the back. The rope was neatly coiled on the floor behind the seats. He dragged it out, had a quick drink from Craig's water bottle, wound the rope over his shoulders and set off back.

His legs were tired, it was baking hot, an ache was building up inside his chest and he was completely knackered. Don't even think about it. Concentrate on relaxing and keeping the stride going.

He reached the foot of the cliff. Take your time, pace yourself, concentrate.

He focused on the steep game trail in front of him, carefully placing his hands and feet, climbing quickly and efficiently.

He reached the top and stood for a moment to orientate and recover his breath. His hands were bleeding, his nails were broken, and there was a graze on one knee where he'd slipped on some loose stones. He barely noticed.

He hitched the rope up on his shoulder and carried on.

Dad and Joel had joined Lucy and Craig at the top of the cliff by the time Kal arrived, breathless and exhausted.

'Well done, Kal,' cried Lucy.

'Man, that was fantastic,' said Craig, handing him a bottle of water.

Kal could only nod. He unwound the rope from his body and dropped it to the ground. Craig picked it up and tied one end to a tree just behind them, then went to the edge of the cliff. 'I'll send the rope down, then we'll haul Matata and Fupi up together.' He shouted the instructions down, and Matata waved back to show he'd understood.

'Kal, can you watch the rope?'

Kal, who had just about recovered, nodded and wriggled to the edge, watching as Craig and Joel paid out the rope. 'Keep going,' he called.

'How much more?' asked Craig.

'Still quite a way yet.'

A flight of mottled swifts swept up the cliff face and wheeled round, their strident cries seeming to jeer the frail humans standing precariously on the edge. Lucy wasn't even aware of them, even though they would have been a new species for her bird list.

'Are we nearly there?' asked Craig.

'The end of the rope's just below the tree,' said Kal.

'Damn,' muttered Craig.

'It's not too short?' cried Lucy.

'By about four metres,' said Kal.

'I'll have to go down,' said Craig. He pulled up the rope and tied the end round his waist. 'Make sure you guys hang on.'

'Craig, no!' cried Kal. 'If you slipped, there's no way we could hold you. And we certainly couldn't pull you back.'

'What, then?'

'I'm the one who has to go. I'm much lighter than you.'

'Kal, you can't!' cried Lucy.

'I can. Besides, I've done some climbing.'

Craig reluctantly untied the rope.

Done some climbing. Are you off your trolley? Two sessions on the climbing wall at the local sports centre where the furthest you could fall was three metres onto spongy matting – not forty metres onto jagged rocks. Kal didn't tell Craig, and he didn't dare look at him as he tied a bowline in the end of the rope and slipped the loop down to his waist. He untied the other end from the tree, took a couple of turns round the trunk and instructed Dad how to belay, by slowly paying out the rope while Craig and Joel lowered him. His mouth felt dry and his muscles like jelly – one of them in his leg wouldn't stop twitching.

'Give me the rucksack,' he said, his voice strangely hoarse. He fitted the rucksack over his back, nodded to Craig and Joel, backed to the edge of the cliff, shut his eyes, opened them again and stepped backwards into space.

Don't look down.

At least, he'd learned the basic techniques of abseiling: lean out from the slope, legs slightly apart, small steps, trust the rope to take your weight. Above all, lean back.

He hoped Dad would remember his one and only lesson in belaying.

Kal moved slowly and easily down the cliff, the rope running smoothly. But what if he slipped out of the loop? He wasn't wearing a harness with twin-safety lines, no helmet, no...

Concentrate. Mat had climbed the whole way without a rope.

Kal's rope caught on a projecting root.

He tried to jerk it free. It wouldn't budge. He looked down. His head swam. He paused waiting for his head to clear. He looked up at the snagged rope, took a deep breath, climbed back up to get some slack, had a brief rest on a projecting rock and shook the rope free.

The rock on which he was standing was suddenly not there.

For a ghastly microsecond, Kal was in free fall.

He cried out as the rope bit into his body, then again as his back slammed against the rock face.

He was vaguely aware of a crash far below as the rock reached the bottom.

'Hang on!' yelled Lucy.

Thanks for the advice. Kal managed to get his feet against

the rock face. He braced them and continued his abseil.

Keep those legs braced. Small steps. Dad, don't forget that belay.

A sudden woosh. Kal felt a stabbing pain in the top of his head. He'd forgotten about the eagles. Something trickled into his eyes blurring his vision. He wiped a hand across his face and licked the saltiness off his lips. Blood. Forget it.

He reached the base of the tree where the eagles were nesting. But Matata and Fupi were still seven metres below. Matata called encouragement but Kal had no idea what he was saying.

He continued down. The rope tightened.

'Can you give me any more?' he yelled up to Lucy.

He was lowered another metre.

'I still can't reach them.'

'Kal. There's nothing left!'

Kal had known the rope was too short. He had just hoped that somehow it might have miraculously lengthened. 'Lucy,' he yelled, 'I'm getting out of the rope.'

There was another woosh. Kal hunched his shoulders and the eagle's talons scraped harmlessly on the rucksack.

Mat had done it. So could he. He slipped the rope off and continued downwards. There were now only the roots of the tree saving him from falling onto those deadly rocks below.

A pigeon shot out of a crevice next to his hand.

Kal screamed.

Then he was beside Matata and Fupi.

Matata grinned. '*Nzuri kabisa* – very awesome!' He would have shaken Kal's hand if he hadn't been clinging onto the tree roots.

Fupi had a nasty gash down her back – probably like the one on Kal's head – but otherwise seemed to be okay.

Kal wiped the blood out of his eyes again, slipped the

rucksack off his back, and he and Matata managed to stuff Fupi into it without falling off. A further struggle, and they fitted the rucksack onto Kal's chest. He closed his eyes for a moment to clear a wave of dizziness.

Fupi licked his face. Yuk – dog spit!

Now, to climb back and get the rope. Or would it be better to climb on down?

He looked down. His eyes swam.

No way!

'Kal, are you okay?'

He was vaguely aware of Lucy's cry.

Never felt better, apart from bleeding to death and clinging to a root no thicker than my little finger.

'You go,' said Matata, pointing to the loop above them.

Kal looked up. How was he going to make it back to that dangling rope? It was swaying gently, seemingly teasing him. It looked more like a hangman's noose than a route to safety. Forget about the rope, focus on the rock face, search out footholds, trust in those flimsy roots.

'Just go,' said Matata. 'I come after.'

Somehow, Kal made it to the base of the tree. He grabbed the rope, managed to slip the loop round the rucksack and over his body. After that, he didn't remember anything else until he felt something running down his face. But this didn't taste salty. It was water – beautiful cool plain water.

'Man, that was just fantastic,' said a familiar voice.

'No sweat.' Kal opened his eyes in time to see a grinning Matata appear over the edge of the cliff, having been hauled up after him.

'Kal, you and Matata were incredible!' Lucy's tear-stained face was wreathed in smiles, as she cradled Fupi in her arms.

'Very well done, you two,' said Dad.

'Nasty scratch but nothing worse,' said Craig, peering at

Kal's head. He trickled some more water over it. 'Fupi's a bit worse, though. That needs stitches.'

'She will be all right?' said Lucy.

'Sure. We'll get her to the vet tomorrow.'

Kal brushed the water out of his eyes, took the bottle from Craig, had a drink then passed it to Matata.

The two boys grinned at each other. 'Cool,' said Kal.

'*Kabisa*!' cried Matata.

They gave each other a high five.

It was almost dark by the time they got back to the plane. Joel and Matata didn't seem in the least dismayed to be staying behind, nor of going back to their place in the dark.

'What's that noise?' asked Lucy.

They all listened. A rasping grunting call was coming from somewhere among the cliffs above them.

'*Chui*,' murmured Matata.

'Leopard,' said Craig.

'But that's where Joel and Matata stay!' cried Lucy.

The two of them grinned.

Lucy shook her head. There was so much to learn about Africa.

'Come on, guys, let's go,' said Craig.

They scrambled into the plane: Kal, Lucy and Fupi in the back, and Dad, nursing his precious bag, sitting in the front with Craig.

Joel and Matata waved and were gone, swallowed up in the darkness.

Craig started the engine, turned the plane onto the strip and switched on the landing lights. They threw ghostly shadows back off the grass and bushes.

Lucy made sure that Fupi was comfortable on her lap then closed her eyes. We can't fail now. There was a bump. Her eyes flew open. Another bump, followed by the familiar sound of the wheels running along the ground. She had slept all the way and now they were safely back.

CHAPTER 8

Bullock cart

THE SECRET DRAWER

Diana scolded Craig for endangering the children, then pronounced Kal fit and well, having washed his wound and applied gentian violet to it. Lucy said it made him look like a punk. An hour later, they were eating dinner.

'Samson's agreed to take Fupi to the vet in the morning,' said Craig.

'Couldn't *you* sew her up?' asked Lucy. 'Like we did with Mondo.'

'I could,' agreed Craig, 'but I want the vet to give her a thorough check. Make sure there's nothing else.'

Lucy nodded. 'Can I go with Samson?'

'Sure, but Faru has an alternative suggestion.'

'Ah, yes.' Faru cleared his throat. 'Craig and I have had a discussion, and we think, now the weather has cleared up, we could fly to the coast tomorrow.'

'And spend Christmas there?' said Lucy, daring to hope.

'I don't see why not,' said Faru. 'Diana has given me the all clear, and…'

'Faru, you must take things easy,' said Diana. 'You had a nasty accident.'

Faru waved a dismissive hand.

'Brilliant!' cried Lucy.

'Right, guys, this is the plan,' said Craig. 'You kids will fly down with Faru tomorrow. Samson and I will get the truck and equipment sorted for the translocation, which will take us a couple of days. Samson will then drive the truck down, taking Martha and Matata. Your mum arrives at the airport on Thursday morning. I'll fly down in my plane with Mother and your dad to meet her and we'll fly on to the coast from there.'

'What about Caspar and Carmen and the other animals?' asked Lucy.

'I'll get two other guys to go into the hills, so Joel can come back and look after them. He won't mind that, he gets paid double for working over Christmas.'

'All fixed, then,' said Faru, rubbing his hands.

'You kids will have an early start tomorrow,' said Dad. 'Better go and get packed.'

They pretended they hadn't heard.

'Dad,' said Lucy, changing the subject, 'did you find some good stuff in the hills?'

'Yes, Lucy, I did.' He got up and fetched the bag he had been nursing so protectively in the plane. 'What you call "stuff" actually contains some splendid examples of ruby – and possibly of even better quality than before.' Dad tipped the contents of his bag onto the table.

By now, all of them, except Faru, had become used to seeing such stones, but they still marvelled at them.

'Did you find all these, Dad?' asked Lucy.

'No, the other two – what were their names?'

'Joel and Matata,' said Craig.

'Ah, yes. They found some of them, but they're not experienced – one couldn't expect it – and most of the better examples were found by me.'

'They are rather lovely,' said Diana, passing one to Faru.

'Beautiful, quite beautiful,' he murmured.

They pored over the stones then Dad scooped them up and returned them to his bag. 'Can you look after them, Craig?'

'Sure, I'll lock them in the safe.'

'We nearly forgot!' cried Lucy. 'Craig, that message.'

'It's in my other shirt,' said Craig. He hurried out and returned a few moments later. 'Ellie, what do you make of that?' he said, passing her the slip of paper.

'Where did this come from?' she cried in amazement.

'The Seki Hills – where we were today?'

'The marks were scratched on the wall of a cliff just near where Matata and Joel are staying,' said Lucy.

'Hang on.' Ellie went off and came back with the atlas. She extracted the previous note from the front and put the two side by side.

'They're not the same,' she said, 'similar, but not identical.'

The others peered over her shoulder.

'It's like opening a wonderful history book,' murmured Ellie, a faraway look in her eyes, 'but one we can't read.'

Kal, under Faru's watchful eye, eased the control column back and the plane lifted off the ground.

'Goodbye, Simba – for a while,' murmured Lucy.

Kal set a course due east. They skirted the Ngorongoro crater and the magnificent dome of Kilimanjaro then passed over several ranges of hills and featureless arid bush. Lucy saw the occasional group of huts and some minute giraffes, and where they crossed a river far below, she could make out tiny animals standing in the water. Kal circled and came in lower and they had a wonderful view of elephants splashing in the river, taking no notice of the plane.

Then, there it was: the place that Lucy had been dreaming about ever since the coast had been mentioned. And it was so much more beautiful than she could have imagined. They flew over a creek where a number of small boats and canoes were anchored. A larger boat was heading out to sea, leaving a ribbon of wake behind it.

Faru turned to the girls. 'That's Watumwani,' he shouted, pointing to a small township at the mouth of the creek.

Lucy nodded and peered ahead. The beautiful Indian Ocean stretched away to the horizon and merged with the clear blue sky above, the only interruption to the view being a small island just below them and two large islands some sixty kilometres off shore.

'The one to the south is Zanzibar,' shouted Faru, 'and the other is Pemba.'

Lucy's eyes widened. 'And the one below?' she asked.

Faru didn't respond, as he was watching Kal who was preparing to land. Below was the turquoise ocean, and just ahead, a line of dazzling coral sand bordered by coconut palms growing where the beach met the land. A white ribbon of surf ran parallel to the beach two hundred metres or so offshore where the fringing coral reef broke up the swell of the ocean.

The coconut palms came nearer. The next thing Lucy knew they were skimming between them and the plane was running easily over the sandy airstrip.

Kal taxied to the end of the strip and switched off the engine.

'Splendid, absolutely splendid, young man,' said Faru.

Kal grinned and opened the door. The baking heat of the coast came flooding in.

'Golly, it's hot,' said Ellie.

'Bit warmer than Simba,' agreed Faru. 'Come on.'

They scrambled out of the plane to see what looked like a chariot coming towards them in a cloud of dust. Two bullocks were galloping along pulling a rickety wooden cart in which a man was standing, bouncing up and down as the cart jolted over bumps. He was holding the animals' tails and urging them on.

Faru waved. 'It's Rashid, my helper,' he said. 'He and his wife Hannah look after me and keep an eye on the place when I'm away.'

The man heaved back on the tails and the bullocks skidded to a halt, panting and snorting. The man jumped down and came over to them. He wore a colourful woven cloth round his waist, and had a T-shirt wrapped round his head. His body glistened with sweat.

'*Karibuni* – welcome,' he cried, smiling as Faru introduced each of the children in turn.

'Come and meet my tractors: Nyati and Mbogo,' said Faru, leading the children across to the bullock cart.

'What do their names mean?' asked Lucy.

Faru chuckled. 'Buffalo and buffalo,' he said. 'Both words mean buffalo in Swahili.'

Lucy stroked the animals' necks, and they rubbed their muzzles against her. 'Come and say hello, Kal,' she called.

'What? And get all that snot rubbed on me. Not likely.' Kal unloaded the bags from the plane and put them in the cart.

'Can I drive?' asked Lucy.

'Of course,' said Faru. 'Rashid will show you what to do.'

Lucy scrambled into the cart, Rashid climbed up beside her and the others clambered in behind. Rashid reached out and picked up the animals' tails. 'One in each hand, *namna hii* – like this.'

Lucy took the tails.

'To turn this way, pull this one,' said Rashid. 'To turn the other way, pull this one. *Sawa* – okay?'

Lucy nodded. 'What happens when I want to stop?'

'Both tails.'

'And to make them go?'

'Just shake.'

Lucy gave a tentative shake and nothing happened.

'More strength,' said Rashid.

Lucy heaved, the bullocks leapt forward and Kal fell out of the back.

'Use the clutch next time!' he yelled. He picked himself out of the sand, caught up the cart and jumped back in.

Lucy ignored him. 'Is this right?' she asked, as the bullocks trotted easily along.

'*Nzuri sana* – very good,' said Rashid. '*Huyu ni fundi*,' he added, turning to Faru.

'What's that?' asked Lucy.

'Rashid says you're an expert.'

She turned and grinned. 'Eco-friendly transport. Imagine going to school like this.'

'You'd have to muck out the bike sheds afterwards,' muttered Kal.

The cart approached a large, slightly untidy building with a roof of coconut palm thatching and walls made out of rough-cut coral blocks that had been whitewashed. The surrounding garden consisted mainly of shrubs and flowering trees.

'What a beautiful place,' said Ellie.

'The lady who used to live here liked flowers,' said Faru, pointing out bougainvillea, flamboyants, bottle-brush trees, hibiscus, and frangipani. 'They are wonderful for the birds.'

Lucy was entranced. Some bewildering new birds flitted amongst the flowers and branches; others were at bird feeders, or bathing in birdbaths, and there was a constant sound of birdsong.

'Hey, where are we going?' cried Kal, as the bullocks continued on past the house.

'Sorry,' said Lucy. She heaved on one of the tails, the cart turned, and this time she remembered to pull both tails to stop.

They jumped down and unloaded their bags. As they walked towards the house, a lady dressed in a brightly coloured wrap-around skirt appeared at the door. She wore green flip-flops on her feet and a colourful scarf round her head.

'That must be Hannah,' Ellie whispered to Lucy. 'The skirt she's wearing is called a *kanga*; everyone wears them at the coast.'

'It looks perfect for such a hot place.'

Ellie nodded. 'I'm sure Faru can tell us where we could buy them.'

The woman came shyly forward and shook everyone's hand. 'My name is Hannah,' she said. 'You are all most welcome.'

'Thank you,' chorused the children.

Hannah's face lit up in a broad smile as Ellie began conversing with her in Swahili.

'What's all that about?' asked Lucy.

'I was admiring her *kanga*,' said Ellie. 'Hannah says we can buy them in the local market; they're not expensive.'

'I didn't come here to spend my time shopping,' grumbled Kal.

'Who's for a swim, then?' cried Faru.

'Me,' said the children, with one voice.

'Splendid. But first let Hannah show you where you're sleeping.'

Five minutes later, Kal was in his swimming things waiting on the veranda for the others. A large brass telescope mounted on a tripod, stood at one end. He went and examined it. Lucy came and joined him.

'How do you like my toy?' asked Faru. He had appeared on the veranda in a pair of bright green baggy shorts with scarlet hibiscus flowers on them.

'Cool,' said Kal. 'May I try it?'

'Of course. When the previous owner of the house died, that was one of the things I inherited '

Kal found the focusing knob, peered through the eyepiece and lined up on a dot in the ocean just beyond the reef. It sprang into his vision and revealed itself as a dugout canoe. The lone fisherman was hauling a net out of the water.

'How did he get across the reef in that?' asked Kal.

'I'll show you.' Faru moved the telescope and focused on the reef. 'There you go.'

Kal peered again. 'There's no surf breaking there,' he said. 'Why's that?'

'A small river – the Sinawe River – comes out just opposite; the fresh water in it prevents the coral growing and leaves what the fisherman call a *mlango* – a door or gateway – in the reef which they can paddle through – quite dangerous though.'

'Why's it dangerous?' asked Lucy.

'Strong currents and sharks sometimes use it.'

'Sharks!'

Faru nodded. 'See that island?' He pointed to the small island that Lucy had seen from the plane.

'What about it?' she asked.

'That's called Papa Island.'

Lucy wrinkled her brow. 'Daddy Island, what's that got to do with things?'

Faru slowly shook his head. 'Not Daddy, Lucy. In Swahili, "*papa*" means shark.'

'Shark?' she whispered.

'The local people tell me that the island is well named. They won't go there.'

'Faru,' said Kal, 'if the sharks come through that *mlango* thing, it means we won't be able to swim.'

'We're fine inside the reef,' said Faru. 'Any sharks that do come through keep to the deep channels, and they always leave before the tide goes down.'

'Better not tell Ellie,' said Lucy. 'She won't believe you.'

Faru chuckled. 'You'll all be quite safe.'

'Ellie, are you coming?' called Kal.

'Just putting on sun cream.'

'Hurry up, the sea will have dried up at this rate.'

'While we're waiting,' said Faru, 'come with me.'

He led Kal and Lucy indoors to a hallway where a magnificent carved wooden chest stood. It was covered in brass scrolls and studs that formed intricate whorls and patterns. There were large handles at each end, elaborate brass hinges for the lid and an imposing clasp on the front.

'Wow!' exclaimed Lucy.

'What do you keep in that,' said Kal, 'the crown jewels?'

Faru chuckled. 'Nothing quite so precious, I'm afraid.'

'Is it old?' asked Lucy.

'I imagine so. This was made in Lamu, an island just off the coast in Kenya. Nowadays, they make cheap copies in Dar es Salaam for the tourists but this is the real thing. Something else I inherited with the house.'

'Cool,' said Kal, running his hands over it and admiring the craftsmanship.

'What's it for?' asked Lucy.

'The Arab merchants and sea captains used them to carry their belongings on voyages,' said Faru.

'I bet the one who owned this was jolly rich,' said Lucy.

'Who knows?'

Ellie joined them. 'Is that a Lamu chest?'

'Rather fine, eh?' said Faru.

'I read about them,' said Ellie. 'Don't they have secret drawers and things?'

Faru smiled. 'I'm told that some of them do.'

'Have you looked for one?' asked Kal.

'Well, er…no. I just use it to keep this stuff in.' Faru lifted the lid, leaned it against the wall and pulled out a very modern plastic box containing flippers and face-masks. 'I keep these for the grandchildren, who visit every other year or so from America,' he said, 'but they should be fine for you.'

Ellie and Lucy rummaged through, but Kal was more interested in the chest, peering all around, pulling out drawers, and tapping the interior.

'Have you found the hidden compartment yet?' asked Ellie.

'With all the treasure and stuff?' added Lucy.

Kal didn't appear to hear. 'Something's not quite right,' he muttered.

'Come on, let's go,' said Ellie. 'What was that about the sea drying up?'

Kal looked up. 'I think I've found something?'

'What?'

'I don't know, but look.' Kal closed the lid of the chest and pulled out three shallow drawers from the base. One contained some old golf balls and a cracked photo frame; another, some secateurs and gardening gloves; and the third one had a pair of sunglasses, a moth-eaten hat, a notebook and a dead mouse.

'Poor thing!' cried Lucy, holding her nose.

'Sorry about that,' said Faru, picking up the shrivelled body and throwing it outside. 'As you can see, all sorts of rubbish gets in here.'

'So where's the treasure?' asked Ellie.

Kal laid the drawers on top of the chest. 'See this drawer, it's the same depth as the chest.' He lined it up with the edges of the lid. 'But these other two are not as deep.'

'Good gracious,' exclaimed Faru, 'I hadn't noticed that – probably only pulled them out one at a time, before.'

'So what, Kal?' said Lucy. 'Perhaps they ran out of wood, or something.'

He gave her a withering look. 'When you design something like this, you don't run out of wood!'

'Sorry.'

'See here,' said Kal.

They bent down and peered where Kal had just removed the drawers.

'These spacers keep the drawers separated.' He indicated two decorated bars of wood that separated the middle drawer from the other two. 'This one is fixed but this one isn't. Let's see.' Kal pulled gently and the spacer bar slid easily out of the recess. 'There you go.'

'Goodness me!' exclaimed Faru.

Attached to the end of the spacer bar was a long narrow drawer. Kal placed this beside the two short drawers and it exactly filled the missing space. But none of the others noticed; they were gazing spellbound a linen cloth roll lying inside the secret drawer.

CHAPTER 9

Lamu chest

THE FOLLOWER

All thoughts of a swim were forgotten as they stared at the roll
of cloth bound with a piece of faded red ribbon.

'Scary,' said Ellie.

'Who would have believed it?' muttered Faru.

Ellie reached out a cautious hand, lifted up the roll, and held
it reverently in her hands.

'Let's see what's inside,' said Lucy.

'I think I should call my archaeologist friend, Abdul Raman,'
said Faru.

'But there might be nothing there,' said Lucy. 'You can hardly
call him and say you've found a dirty bit of cloth in an old chest.'

Faru nodded. 'All right, but we must be very careful.' He led
them to the dining room table, and they pulled up chairs. 'You
do it, my dear,' he said to Ellie. 'I'm too nervous.'

'Are you sure?'

Faru nodded.

Ellie slowly untied the ribbon.

They watched, mesmerized, as she unrolled the cloth. A wonderful aroma of exotic spices wafted into the air.

'There's nothing there,' said Lucy. 'I told you.'

'Wait.' Ellie had unrolled the cloth, but the edges were still folded into the middle. She carefully laid them back to reveal two sheets of yellowed parchment. One was covered in faded writing and the other appeared to be a diagram with notes written on it. 'Look at that,' she whispered.

'I'm calling Abdul,' said Faru, and disappeared into the sitting room. They could hear his muffled voice on the phone as they continued to gaze in wonder at the parchments.

'Looks like the same sort of writing as we found in the caves,' said Kal.

Ellie nodded. 'I'll go and get the messages, so we can compare.'

She and Faru returned together.

'Abdul is most excited,' said Faru. 'He's coming straight away. In the meantime, he says not to touch the paper or we could damage it.'

Ellie laid the two messages beside the old papers. 'The writing looks the same,' she said.

'Definitely Arabic,' muttered Faru, peering closely.

'And that diagram could be some sort of map,' said Kal.

Ellie nodded. 'I think so.'

After their initial excitement, there was no more to be done until Abdul arrived. Ellie began making notes on a pad she had brought from her room, Kal went back to examining the chest, while Faru and Lucy took cold drinks out to the veranda and sat admiring the view and watching the birds.

When an elderly Peugeot car drew up beside the house an hour later, Ellie and Kal were still engrossed in their self-appointed tasks, and Lucy, with Faru's help, had identified six new species of bird, including a magnificent red and green Fischer's touraco that came to the birdbath only a few paces from the veranda.

The man who climbed out of the vehicle reminded Lucy of a bird; he had alert darting eyes, a manner to match, and a large beaky nose on which was perched a pair of glasses that kept slipping down. He came bustling onto the veranda carrying a small briefcase.

'Faru,' he cried, 'what's all this? Most exciting. And this is one of the young ladies you mentioned?' He held out his hand to Lucy.

'Hello,' said Lucy.

'Yes,' said Abdul, nodding and pushing his glasses back up his nose. 'In here, are we?' He led the way into the dining room.

Ellie rose, smiled and held out her hand. '*Salaam alaikum.*'

'*Wa alaikum as salaam*,' responded Abdul automatically, then blinked. 'Good gracious!' he cried. 'You speak Arabic?'

'Not really, only the greetings.'

'Well, well.' Abdul beamed, took off his glasses and polished them on his shirt.

'Hey, guys, come and look at this,' came Kal's voice from the hallway.

They went through and found Kal sitting on the floor, peering at the underside of the metal flap that secured the lid of the chest. 'It looks like some sort of writing. I'm Kal,' he added, when he saw Abdul.

'Quite so,' said Abdul. 'Now, what have we here?'

Kal held up the metal flap and pointed.

Abdul pushed his glasses onto his forehead and peered at the faint marks. Then he opened his briefcase, pulled out a magnifying glass and peered again at the marks. He gave a sharp intake of breath.

'What does it say, Abdul?' asked Faru.

Abdul's eyes were shining. 'It says: "*Praise be to Allah, Suleiman Sulman*".' He stood up, and appeared to notice the chest for the first time. He ran his hands lovingly over the surface. 'You don't see many of these nowadays. Where did you get it, Faru?'

'I inherited it with the house.'

Abdul nodded. 'You've got it insured?'

'Er,' said Faru. 'I just use it to store the goggles and flippers in.'

Abdul looked scandalised. 'Faru, this could be worth thousands of pounds!'

'Goodness gracious!' Faru sat down on the chest but hastily got up again when he saw Abdul's disapproving look. 'I've got to keep those things somewhere,' he muttered.

Abdul tutted.

'Abdul,' said Ellie, 'do you know anything about… what was his name?'

'Suleiman Sulman?'

'Yes, him.'

Abdul nodded. 'He was not a nice man. He was a slave trader who gathered up slaves and sent them off to the Middle East.'

'That's horrible,' said Lucy.

Ellie peered at the writing on the metal flap. 'Did he ever go inland?' she asked.

'Oh yes.' Abdul nodded and had to grab his glasses. 'Records suggest he went as far as the great inland sea – what we now call Lake Victoria.'

'Would he have gone anywhere near Mount Kilimanjaro?'

'Quite possibly.'

Ellie's eyes lit up. 'Come,' she said, and led Abdul back to the dining room. She indicated the scraps of paper. 'I think the name on the chest is the same.'

Everyone stared at her.

Abdul peered at the two notes. 'Ah,' he squeaked. Now, he was the one who needed to sit down. He looked up, a stunned expression on his face. 'It *is* the same name,' he whispered.

Hannah came and said that lunch was ready but Ellie and Abdul were so engrossed in the documents that neither noticed. Faru, Kal and Lucy went out to the veranda, and Ellie was vaguely aware of their voices and occasional laughter, but her mind was being led back some hundred and fifty years.

Abdul slowly translated the messages from the caves while Ellie copied down what he said. Then he put on a pair of fine linen gloves and transferred his attention to the two documents. Ellie's excitement was growing all the time. The diagram *was* a map, but it was crudely drawn, and the only measurements given were distances walked in a day – somewhere between five and ten miles. Rivers and lakes were marked because they were sources of fresh water, and there was a blob labelled the "mountain of white rock", and another labelled the "great bowl". Some place names were marked, among them Watumwani.

'So, Sulman came here?' said Ellie.

'Almost certainly. Watumwani means the "place of slaves". The slavers travelled all along the East African coast, even as far south as Mozambique.' He indicated the map. 'As you can see, most of the place names lie along the coastline but very few are shown inland.'

'I know it was a horrible trade but it does sound romantic,' said Ellie.

'Opening up the Dark Continent, bringing the gospel to its people, building the Empire, that sort of thing?'

Ellie nodded.

Abdul polished his glasses. 'British historians and missionaries tried to portray it like that, but I'm afraid it wasn't in the least romantic. It was barbaric, savage and extremely unpleasant, with diseases, wild animals, warlike tribes and lack of water, all adding to the hazards. People who weren't well armed and well prepared usually perished very quickly. Those who had firearms – the Arabs – were on top; those who did not – most of the indigenous people – were forced into slavery. It was a most shameful period.'

'Oh,' said Ellie, feeling abashed. 'What about the missionaries?'

'Most of them died before they got more than a few miles inland.'

'That's awful.'

'Usually malaria – I hope you're taking your anti-malarial tablets, by the way.'

Ellie nodded.

'Then there were the local tribes who killed all outsiders without distinguishing between slave traders, explorers or missionaries. A few missionaries did make it to the interior but often found themselves having to get help or protection from the armed slave traders – the people whose trade they were trying to abolish.'

Ellie shook her head in disbelief.

Abdul gave a faint smile. 'Ironic, isn't it? Even the great Dr Livingstone was helped on several occasions by one of the most notorious slave traders of the day, a man called Muhammad el Marjebi – better known as Tipu Tip. He saved Livingstone's life more than once.'

Ellie could have listened to this fascinating history all day.

'Come, let's return to the map,' said Abdul, giving his glasses another polish. 'Many of the places marked on the coast were where the dhows – the ships of that time – could get through the reef and moor to pick up slaves, ivory and spices, which were then shipped north to Oman, Arabia and such like.' He indicated several points on the map, including Watumwani. 'But as the anti-slave movement gathered momentum, particularly in England, the slavers could no longer work openly and had to hide their slaves.'

'How?'

'Mostly using caves that had access to the sea.'

'Couldn't the slaves escape?'

'I'm sure a lot of them tried, but don't forget they were probably chained together and very few of them would have been able to swim.'

'How awful!'

Ellie saw sadness in his eyes.

'The people who conducted that terrible trade – my ancestors – have much to answer for.' He cleared his throat. 'Enough. I think we should tell the others what we have discovered.'

'My assistant has been extremely helpful,' said Abdul, when the others had returned to the dining room. 'I'll let her tell you.'

'Have some lunch first,' said Faru. 'We've saved you some.'

'Most kind,' said Abdul, 'but not for me.'

'I'm not hungry,' said Ellie. 'It's all too exciting.'

'Tell us, Ellie,' said Lucy.

Abdul smiled and nodded encouragingly.

Ellie took a deep breath. 'Right, as Abdul says, the messages in the caves, the map, and this paper with the writing on it, all appear to have been written by the same person – a man called Suleiman Sulman. He was a trader who came from Oman – that's in the Middle East. Is that right?' She looked at Abdul.

He smiled and nodded. 'Yes, and it appears that Faru's splendid chest used to belong to him.'

'What an amazing coincidence,' exclaimed Faru.

Ellie continued. 'Although the paper talks about several journeys Sulman made, getting ivory and slaves and things, the map – and the notes written on it – describe only one, a journey to the "mountain of white rock" and the "great bowl".'

'What are they?' said Lucy.

'The mountain of white rock is undoubtedly Mount Kilimanjaro,' said Abdul. 'People in those days didn't realise that snow could exist on the equator. They thought it could only be rock.'

'And the great bowl?'

'That's a bit more of a puzzle,' said Abdul, stroking his chin. He looked round at the others. 'Any ideas?'

'Ellie,' said Lucy, 'what's the name of that crater we fly over just near Simba?'

'You reckon Sulman was flying?' said Kal. 'What – on his magic carpet?'

'No, of course not. But that crater does look like a bowl.'

'Ngorongoro crater!' cried Faru.

'Of course.' said Abdul. 'Even from the ground it looks like a great bowl, and I believe there is permanent water there. Well done, Lucy.'

Lucy blushed. 'So why did Sulman go there?' she asked.

'It seems that he was following someone,' said Ellie. 'Sulman doesn't give a name, he just says he was called the Follower.'

'That doesn't make sense,' said Lucy, 'following the Follower.'

Abdul nodded. 'That's how the text translates.'

'The Follower, you say?' said Faru, wrinkling his brow and rubbing a hand over his hair.

'Sulman also talks about another follower…'

'This is really confusing,' said Lucy.

'It's easy,' said Kal, 'it's a follower following someone who's following a follower. Right?'

Ellie grinned. 'Right.'

'Glad you can follow it.'

Lucy groaned.

'Listen,' said Ellie, 'Sulman gives the name of the man who was with him, *his* follower; he was called Punyura.' She looked to Abdul for confirmation.

He nodded.

'It seems that Punyura had been a slave but Sulman released him.'

'So Sulman wasn't all bad?' said Kal.

'No, indeed,' said Abdul, in a husky voice. They all looked at him. 'You must excuse me,' he said.

'Are you all right, Abdul?' asked Faru. 'Can I get you some water or something?'

Abdul blinked a few times and shook his head. 'Go on, Ellie.'

'Well,' she continued, 'it seems that this Punyura came from somewhere near the great bowl – Ngorongoro crater – and was part of a slave caravan that had been captured by Sulman. According to the manuscript, lions attacked the caravan one night and Sulman was badly mauled and lost part of one arm. Most of the slaves escaped and fled but Punyura managed to drive off the lions. He stayed with Sulman all night and next day carried him to a cave…'

'A cave!'

Ellie's face was radiant. 'You won't believe this but it was the cave we stayed in! The message we found was scratched on the wall by Sulman.'

'Wow,' breathed Lucy.

Ellie hurried on. 'They stayed there many nights and eventually Sulman, having been cared for by the slave, recovered but…'

'What did you say the guy's name was?' asked Kal.

'Sulman's rescuer?'

'Yeah.'

'He was called Punyura.'

'Punyura, and he came from near the Ngoro… whatsit?'

'Kal, what are you getting at?' asked Ellie.

'Mat's dad – that's what!'

'Have you flipped?' said Lucy. 'What's Matata's dad got to do with…?' Her voice trailed off. 'Matata's dad was called…'

'Punyua!' cried Kal. 'I bet, with a name like that, it could be a relation, an ancestor or something. Is that right, Abdul?'

'Who is Matata?' asked Abdul.

Ellie explained.

Abdul took off his glasses and blinked. 'The pronunciation is slightly different but that is probably immaterial. I think they could well be related.'

'Definitely,' said Faru. 'In our culture, someone who had saved a person from lions would be very famous. Such a story would be recounted many times and his name would live on.'

'Mat's not afraid of lions,' said Kal. He reminded them of the time he and Matata had been running with Reuben, and how Matata had chased off a lion that had threatened them. 'So he's probably inherited his great great great grandfather's – or whoever's – courage.'

Faru nodded vigorously. 'Exactly so.'

Abdul bobbed his head like an excited sparrow. 'It is findings like these that make history come alive.'

'Certainly more interesting than learning the dates of the kings and queens of England,' muttered Kal.

'I wish we had a famous relative,' said Lucy wistfully.

'There is Bramwell Bartlett,' said Ellie. 'Dad said he was famous.'

'Bartlett's bantams!' cried Kal. 'Who wants an ancestor who bred poxy chickens?'

'Kal, it doesn't matter,' said Ellie. 'Anyway,' she continued, 'Sulman was so grateful to Punyura for saving his life that he vowed never again to take part in slavery and promised the

Follower that, from now on, he would work to abolish it.'

'Who is this Follower dude?' asked Kal.

'I think he was some mystical figure whom Sulman was following,' said Abdul, 'probably not a real person.'

'It's weird,' said Kal.

'It may seem weird to us,' said Abdul, 'but you must remember, in those days people's lives were governed by all kinds of mysticism, fortune telling and omens, and some things that Sulman recounts should not be taken too literally.'

'What's in the second message we found?' asked Lucy.

'That *is* weird,' said Ellie. She leafed through her notes. 'Here we are. This one reads: *The Follower led me to the tomb, and from here I found where his tears had fallen, and became a rich man.*'

Kal shook his head. 'That certainly doesn't make sense.'

Abdul wagged a finger. 'No, no. Perhaps not to us but it would have made sense to Sulman. We just have to work out what it means.'

'Are you sure you've translated it right?' asked Lucy.

Abdul frowned at her over his glasses.

She blushed. 'Sorry.'

Faru cleared his throat. 'I er... may have a suggestion about this er... Follower person.'

'What?' they all cried.

'It's getting late,' said Faru. 'We should have dinner – you'll stay, Abdul?'

'Well I really ought to...'

'Splendid.'

None of them had realised how quickly the time had flown. Now it was almost dark outside.

'Faru,' said Lucy, 'you still haven't told us about the Follower.'

'All in good time, Lucy, but first I must tell Hannah that we'll be one extra for dinner.'

CHAPTER 10

Telescope

ALL IN THE STARS

They ate dinner on the veranda, looking out over the deep blue
Indian Ocean with the lights from Zanzibar and Pemba twinkling
in the distance, and the murmur of surf washing over the reef
providing a background of soothing sound. Faru had lit two
pyrethrum smoke coils that were burning at each end of the
veranda to keep the mosquitoes at bay.

Ellie turned to him. 'Faru, please tell us about the Follower.'

'Just be patient, my dear.' He refused to be drawn. Instead,
he and Abdul told the children stories about the coast and its
early settlement by Arabs, and about the villages they established,
some of which had grown into flourishing towns, while others
had been abandoned, overtaken by forest and forgotten.

'What about the ruins on the reserve?' asked Kal.

'They're supposed to be near the Sinawe River – over there.'
Faru pointed into the darkness. 'But it's all overgrown; I've never
been there.'

'Are the ruins haunted?' asked Lucy.

Faru chuckled. 'I'm sure the local people will tell you that.
Probably so I don't go there upsetting their poaching.'

'Can we go and look?'

'Wait till Craig comes. Wouldn't want you going in there on
your own – snakes and things, you know.'

'You should come with us, Abdul,' said Lucy.

'Yes, indeed.' Abdul nodded and beamed round. 'There are
unconfirmed reports of an ancient Arab village near here, which
would certainly make sense with a source of fresh water nearby.'
He looked at his watch. 'Goodness, is that the time?'

'You can't go,' said Lucy. 'Faru hasn't told us about the
Follower yet.'

'Ah yes, the Follower.' Faru looked into the darkness. 'Just
about right, now.' He got up from his seat, went to the end of the
veranda, picked up his telescope, carried it onto the lawn away
from the lights of the house and lined it up on the sky. 'There,' he
said. 'Take a look, Lucy. What do you see?'

'It's a fuzzy dot,' said Lucy, peering through the eyepiece. 'I
suppose it's a star or something, but what's it got to do with the
Follower?'

'Can I look?' asked Kal, pushing Lucy aside. 'It looks reddish.'

'Good,' said Faru. 'Ellie?'

'Is it a star or a planet?' she asked.

'A star,' said Faru. 'Abdul, do you want to look?'

The starlight was so bright that they could see Abdul clearly.
He was smiling and shaking his head. 'I confess, Faru, that I have
been rather foolish. I imagine the star that you are showing us is
Aldebaran.'

'That's it.'

'How do you know, if you haven't looked?' said Lucy.

'Aldebaran, or as we would say in Arabic: *al-dabaran*, means the Follower.'

'The follower!' cried Ellie. 'So Sulman was following a star.'

'Exactly. I should have realised but I confess I was rather distracted,' said Abdul, nodding to himself.

'Distracted by what?' asked Lucy.

'I er... perhaps I should explain.' Abdul paused. 'My full name is Abdul bin Sulman Rahman.'

'Sulman Rahman?' said Ellie. 'You're related to Suleiman Sulman!'

Abdul nodded. 'I must say this whole experience has been very moving.' He blew his nose. 'The slave trade was a terrible episode in the history of my ancestors – perhaps that explains why I feel so compelled to research it.' He gave a sigh. 'I cannot say how pleased I am that the documents you have shown me go some way to clearing the name of at least one member of my family.'

'Gracious me,' muttered Faru.

'Faru, you must think me very foolish.'

'Not at all, my friend. I'm glad my little hobby has some uses.'

'Tell us about the star, Abdul,' said Ellie.

Abdul smiled. 'I'm sure you know the story of the three wise men from the east.'

'Oh yes,' said Lucy. 'They followed the star that led them to Bethlehem.'

'Precisely. Although it probably wasn't a star, it was undoubtedly some heavenly body – possibly a comet. The wise men were navigating in the way that all the Arab travellers and sailors did at that time. The Arabs gave names to all the bright stars in the sky – many names that we still use today.'

'Why's this one called the Follower?' asked Ellie.

'Faru, you tell her,' said Abdul.

Faru pointed into the myriad of bright stars overhead. 'See that cluster of stars there. My people call them *Nyuki* – the Bees.'

'Are they what we call the Seven Sisters?' said Ellie.

'That's right. And that star below them, that's Aldebaran, the Follower, the one we've been looking at. It always appears to follow the Bees or Seven Sisters, hence its name.'

'Why's it reddish?' asked Kal, who was peering again through the telescope.

'It's a dying star; what astronomers call a red giant,' said Faru.

'I didn't know stars died,' said Lucy.

'Oh yes, takes millions of years though. When they've burned up all their fuel, the temperature falls – that's why they turn red – and they start expanding. Aldebaran is about forty five times bigger than our sun.'

'It must be enormous!' cried Lucy.

'It is indeed. One of the brightest stars in the sky,' said Faru. 'It lies in the constellation called Taurus.'

'*Al taur*,' murmured Abdul.

'The bull,' said Ellie.

'I can't see a bull,' said Kal.

'Nor can I,' admitted Faru, 'but Aldebaran is supposed to be its eye.'

'The bull's-eye!' cried Kal. 'I like it.'

'It is believed to bring good fortune and riches to anyone who follows it,' said Abdul.

'It seemed to work for Sulman,' said Ellie. 'Didn't he say he became a rich man?'

'Indeed.'

'He hit the bull's eye and won the jackpot,' cried Kal.

Ellie groaned. 'Wasn't it something about the tears of the Follower?'

92

'I found where his tears had fallen, and became a rich man,' quoted Abdul. 'That's what the text says, but I don't…'

'Look!' cried Lucy. 'Shooting star. Make a wish, everyone.'

The brilliant streak seemed to dive into the sea.

'Let's follow it,' said Lucy. She had become bored with astronomy. 'Perhaps *we'll* find good fortune and riches.'

'Dream on,' said Kal.

'Can we follow it, Faru? Can we have our swim in the dark?'

'Why not?' cried Faru. 'The tide will be in now. Let's go.'

'I must be leaving,' said Abdul.

'Far too late, Abdul, you'll have to stay the night.'

'Well, I really…'

'Splendid! We'll go back to the house and I'll ask Hannah to get the spare room ready.'

Abdul, although he agreed to stay the night, absolutely refused to swim. Now that the Follower had been identified, he wanted to see what other mysteries might be hidden in Sulman's map and messages.

Ellie was very torn between staying and swimming, but decided to swim.

Faru found torches for them, and they followed him along a narrow path that led to the beach below. Lucy cried out in amazement. Thousands of pairs of eyes were illuminated by the torchlight.

'What are they?' whispered Ellie.

'Ghost crabs,' said Faru.

'Do they bite?'

'They might if you were able to catch one. Go on, Kal, show us.'

'What! And have a finger taken off? Not likely.'

Faru chuckled. 'Would only be a nip.'

Kal darted after one of the crabs. It scuttled off, and dived into a hole. He tried to catch another. It did the same. Kal put down his torch. 'Right, guys, shine the torches for me.'

This time Kal meant business, but no matter how quick he was, the crabs were quicker, scuttling off, or diving down holes. He didn't even touch one.

'There, Ellie,' said Faru. 'I think we'll be safe.'

They kept on their trainers and waded into the sea. The waves were lapping gently on the white sand, and the water was crystal clear and wonderfully warm – almost like a bath, thought Lucy. She could just make out ghostly shapes slipping and darting through the shallows. 'What are they, Faru?'

'Stingrays.'

Ellie leapt out of the water.

'It's all right, Ellie, they're even more wary than the ghost crabs.'

'Are you sure?'

'Never been stung in all the time I've been swimming here.'

'It's brilliant,' cried Kal, setting off with a powerful crawl.

'Keep over the sand,' called Faru. 'You can use the dinghy to explore further out when it's light.' He pointed to a small boat that was moored to a nearby buoy.

They splashed and swam in the warm water then lay back in the shallows. The moon was just rising and illuminating the whiteness of the surf where the Indian Ocean washed against the reef, whispering as it did so – its sound mingling with the background buzz of cicadas.

'This is just so beautiful,' said Lucy.

'You can understand why people followed stars,' murmured Ellie. 'Look how clear and bright they are.'

'Is that the bull's-eye?' asked Kal, pointing upwards.

'That's it,' said Faru.

'Let's hope it will lead us to…' Lucy stopped. 'There's someone watching us.'

'Where?' said Kal.

'There, look.' Lucy pointed down the beach.

'I can't see anyone.'

'He's gone.'

'Yeah, right,' said Kal. 'Probably the life guard to say it's illegal to swim after dark.'

'Don't believe me, then! But there *was* someone.'

'Who would it have been, Faru?' asked Ellie.

'Probably a fisherman; they sometimes put traps out at night. Although the shoreline and inside the reef are still part of the reserve, I allow local people to fish using their traditional methods.'

'Is there a path down to the beach, there?'

'Nothing – only thick forest. That's where the Sinawe River comes out.'

'Can boats go up it,' asked Kal, 'canoes and things?'

'Only a little way, then the forest closes in.'

'I'm going to explore,' said Lucy.

'Not tonight,' said Faru. 'Time to go in now.'

CHAPTER 11

Elephant-shrew

THE PATH IN THE FOREST

The children found it so hot at night, particularly under mosquito nets, that it was difficult to sleep, and they were up as soon as it was light. They put on their swimming things and – taking Faru's advice – trainers and T-shirts. Lucy took her bag with her binoculars and bird book. It seemed strange not to have Fupi trotting at her heels.

When they got to the beach the air was still, there wasn't a cloud in the sky, and everywhere was bathed in the pink glow of dawn. A few birds were probing in the sand at the water's edge and the ghost crabs were standing guard outside their holes – still just as wary. Two fishermen in dugout canoes were heading towards the break in the reef – the *mlango*. The children waved and the men waved back.

Lucy looked to where she had seen the man last night, but there was no sign of him or anyone else. They had the beach completely to themselves.

The tide was much further out now, exposing shallows and

rock pools, and Faru's dinghy was resting on the sand. The water wasn't deep enough for swimming, so the children wandered along in the shallows peering into pools and marvelling at the strange and beautiful underwater life: hermit crabs hidden in abandoned shells, fat ugly sea cucumbers, bizarre-looking cushion starfish, sea urchins with four-inch spines (a good reason to keep one's trainers on), and brilliant fish that darted off as they approached. When they waded into deeper water, they found coral growing in a bewildering variety of shapes and colours. Out here, the fish were even more beautiful, with colours ranging through the entire spectrum of the rainbow. It was a new world to all of them, and Lucy felt as bemused by the astonishing variety as she had when she had first seen the African birds.

They were now glad of their T-shirts because the sun had risen straight up out of the sea and was already beating down on them much more strongly than they were used to.

'It'll soon be deep enough for swimming,' said Ellie. They had been so enthralled they had hardly noticed the rising water, which was already up to their waists.

'Let's take Faru's boat out,' said Kal. He waded over to the dinghy, which was now floating in a metre of water, untied the rope from the mooring buoy and scrambled in. Ellie followed.

'Look,' she cried, 'it's got a glass bottom. Everything's really clear.'

'You coming, Lucy?' asked Kal, as he fitted the oars in place.

'Later. I'm going to explore.' Lucy waded back to the beach.

'It'll be breakfast soon,' called Ellie.

Lucy waved, kicked off her shoes and walked bare-foot along the hot sand, scuffing it up as she went and swinging her bag. She looked back. Kal was rowing the dinghy slowly out towards the reef and Ellie was peering through the glass bottom. Lucy could hear her frequent cries of delight as she saw something new.

Lucy reached the end of the beach and came to a rocky ledge, below which was a deep channel that connected directly to the sea. This must be where that river came in. She couldn't remember its name. The advancing tide washed against the ledge and surged up the channel, creating treacherous currents that swirled and eddied amongst the rocks. Large shapes were swimming in the depth. Lucy's eyes widened; could they be sharks that had come through the reef?

The channel or creek was about twenty metres wide, and on its far side was thick forest out of which grew a number of coconut palms. On the landward side, the channel disappeared round a bend in an overhanging cliff that was also covered in impenetrable forest.

Lucy could go no further.

She sat down on a rock with her back to the cliff and watched some bright yellow birds chattering away amongst the trees on the other side of the channel. The birds were stripping fibres out of the coconut fronds and using them to weave beautiful intricate nests on the swaying branches of a tree. She pulled her binoculars out of the bag. The birds were clearly weavers, but which ones? She thumbed through the book and eventually separated them from the other similar weavers; they were golden palm weavers. Beautiful. She returned the binoculars and the book to her bag, leaned back, closed her eyes and listened to the gentle sounds all around: the murmur of the surf on the reef, the buzzing of cicadas, the chattering of the weavers and the lapping of the water in the channel.

She awoke with a start to a strange banging noise. She looked around in alarm.

A dugout canoe emerged from round the bend in the creek. The man in it was paddling frantically, the paddle banging against the side of the canoe with each stroke.

Lucy called to him.

He looked in her direction but gave no indication that he had seen or heard her. He simply continued to paddle furiously out to sea.

She felt a sudden chill. The man's face held a look of absolute terror. A shiver ran down her back as she stared after him.

A wave washed over her feet. She leapt up. The ledge on which she had been sitting was surrounded by angry swirling water. Another wave coiled round her feet, like some malevolent snake threatening to drag her into that menacing channel. She searched desperately around but there was no way up the cliff or through the forest. She was cut off.

Kal rowed out near the reef and could see, that what from the shore looked harmless and innocent, was actually hostile and dangerous. The rising tide was breaking over the reef and there was the ominous throb of pounding waves. He kept well clear, then shipped the oars and let the dinghy drift on the incoming tide while he and Ellie peered through the glass bottom.

'It's like a massive aquarium,' said Ellie.

'Look!' cried Kal, indicating a pair of enormous jaws poking out of a crevice in the rock. 'I wouldn't want to mess with him. What is it?'

'Looks like some sort of eel,' said Ellie. 'Look there!' They were drifting over an outcrop of mauve coral, around which were scores of black-and-white-striped fish.'

'Newcastle supporters,' murmured Kal.

As the shadow of the boat passed over the coral, the fish darted into the safety of its branches.

'Any sign of Lucy?' asked Ellie.

Kal looked up. 'No, she's probably gone into breakfast. Let's go.' He fitted the oars in place and rowed back. The water was now too deep to stand and Kal had to lean over the prow to tie the dinghy to the buoy. They then dived over the side, swam to shore and ran up to the house for breakfast.

Lucy was not there.

Lucy was getting frantic. Would she be able to get back to dry land, or would she have to wait for the water to go down? Perhaps the water wouldn't go down; it would just go on rising. All thoughts of the man in the canoe were forgotten. She searched along the ledge where she was marooned. There was no way off – and the tide was still rising. She would have to swim and hope she could keep her bag dry. More importantly, she would have to risk the sharks or whatever they were she had seen swimming in the depths. There was no choice. Besides, sharks only attacked if there was blood in the water. 'I'm sure that's the case,' she said out loud. But she wasn't sure. She looked at the surging water, gritted her teeth and took a tentative step forward. Another snake-like wave coiled round her feet and swirled away to the deep water of the channel. She couldn't risk it. Perhaps there was an undertow that would suck her down, or a current that would sweep her away and smash her against the reef. Then, she really would be bleeding. A dark shape seemed to flash past in the depths. Lucy shivered, despite the heat of the day. She turned away from the channel and looked at the cliff behind. It consisted of jagged coral rock that was undercut at the base then rose straight up for some six or seven metres before disappearing into fringing forest. Kal might have been able to find a way to climb it, but there was no way she could find even a foothold. She gave a sudden start. A man stood watching her. Where on earth had he come from? He was dressed in a turban and a long white robe. It was the man she had seen last night. She *hadn't* imagined it.

'*Jambo*,' she said.

The man nodded and smiled.

'How are you?'

The man nodded again.

Lucy tried Swahili. '*Habari yako?*'

The man's expression didn't change.

'I'm afraid I don't speak Arabic,' said Lucy, realising why he wasn't responding.

The man looked friendly enough, but Lucy began to feel uneasy. 'I've got to go now,' she said. But where?

She looked again at the swirling water and the cliff face. There was just no way. But where had the man come from? He must know a way. She looked again at the dangerous water. The man shook his head and indicated that she should follow him. There was no alternative.

'Where are we going?' she asked.

The man continued to smile.

Smile; that's all he seems to do. Perhaps he can't talk; perhaps he's dumb. She pointed to her mouth and made what she thought might be appropriate gestures.

The man made no response, other than smiling more widely. He then turned towards the forest at the edge of the creek and disappeared.

Lucy followed. There *was* a path. She hadn't looked properly. The man was just ahead, walking up a steep but very obvious path. Lucy scrambled after him. As soon as they were clear of the fringing undergrowth, the path levelled off and the forest opened out, but it was oppressively hot away from the cooling breeze of the sea. The man strode away ahead of her.

'Wait,' she called.

There was a skittering in the leaves. Lucy jumped. A golden brown animal scampered off. It was about the size of Fupi, but more slender, and had a sharp turned-up nose for snuffling amongst the leaves. It clearly wasn't an antelope, it wasn't one of the small carnivores like a civet or genet, and it certainly wasn't any sort of pig. Before she could get her binoculars out, the animal was gone.

The man had stopped and was watching her, an amused expression on his face.

'I need to get back,' said Lucy, 'home, back.' She remembered the Swahili word for house: 'Nyumba, home, house. Me go.'

The man nodded and turned. Lucy continued after him.

They came round a bend in the path and there in front were a number of very old buildings that blended perfectly with the forest around. They were built of coral rock and their roofs were made from coconut fronds. The man stopped outside one with a beautifully carved wooden door that lay open. Inside, it was quite dark.

The man smiled and pointed along the track indicating the way.

'Thank you so much for helping me,' she said. 'Thank you, asante sana.' She held out her hand, and then felt a real idiot. The poor man had lost his right arm, and here she was trying to shake hands. Why hadn't she noticed? What a twit!

The man didn't seem in the least offended. He just smiled and gave a slight bow.

She heard laughter and a voice. It sounded like Rashid. Perhaps he'd come to find her.

'Goodbye – kwa heri. Thank you for rescuing me. Asante sana.' She ran towards the sound of the laughter. Ahead she could see an enormous tree with a great swollen trunk. The forest thinned out, and the path led past the tree and into a field where some animals were grazing. She turned to wave but the man was gone. The little animal with the pointy nose had reappeared and was sniffing the air in her direction.

Lucy suddenly remembered: an elephant-shrew. It was just like Faru had described.

The animals in the field looked up as Lucy appeared. One of them snorted. They looked like some sort of antelope, but not one that she had ever seen before – and they were big, about the size of small horses. Roan antelope. Of course – the whole reason we've come to the coast. The antelope had sandy-coloured coats and black and white faces, but most striking were the sweeping horns that curved towards their backs. One of the animals tossed its head and trotted off. The rest of the herd followed. They're rather handsome, thought Lucy, as she walked towards a large stockade where she could see three men, one of whom was Rashid. They were sitting laughing, chatting, and chewing sugarcane. Nyati and Mbogo, who were harnessed in their cart, stood under a nearby mango tree, munching sugar cane tops. The men looked startled when Lucy appeared.

'Hello,' she called, 'were you looking for me? I got cut off by the tide and had to come back through the forest.' She thought she'd better not mention the man in case he'd been a poacher or something.

'Which way did you come?' asked Rashid.

'That way.' Lucy pointed.

The men glanced at one another.

Rashid smiled and shook his head. 'Not possible.'

'I did. I came out by that big…' Her voice trailed off. She could make out a big tree, but it was surrounded by thick forest and there was a barbed wire fence between the forest and the field. She looked wildly around. There appeared to be no breaks in the vegetation or the fence, and certainly no path.

'I'm sure it was…'

Rashid murmured something to the other two men and they looked uneasy.

'Lucy, I will take you back,' said Rashid.

'I tell you, I *did* come through the forest.'

'The sun is very hot, Lucy.'

He doesn't believe me. None of them believe me. All right, I'll come back here with Craig, and we'll find the path.

'Come,' said Rashid. He led Lucy over to the cart. There were some empty sacks in the back of it. 'This is the place where we feed those ones,' said Rashid, indicating the roan herd. 'They are now getting used to people.'

'Oh,' said Lucy, and climbed into the cart.

Although Rashid tried to engage her in conversation, she was too preoccupied to respond except with monosyllables. Suddenly, her confused thoughts were swept away as a plane roared overhead. She looked up. Craig was just coming in to land.

'Rashid,' she cried, 'we must go and meet them.' She grabbed the two tails from him, urged the protesting bullocks into a gallop and raced towards the plane.

CHAPTER 12

Dugout canoe

THE CANOE

When they reached the plane, Craig was just climbing out.

'Hi, Lucy, how's it going?'

'Brilliant! This is such a brilliant place.'

He grinned.

'Lucy, darling, how are you?' called Mum, as she struggled out of the little plane. She gave Lucy a hug and looked around. 'What a heavenly spot.'

'Mum, it's fabulous. We're having a fantastic time.'

'I know someone who's looking forward to seeing you,' said Craig. He lifted Fupi out and set her on the ground.

The little dog gave a bark of excitement and did a few circuits around Lucy before allowing herself to be picked up. Lucy examined her back. The hair had been clipped away and there was a neat line of stitches where, last time Lucy had seen her, was a horrible gaping wound.

'Is she going to be all right, Craig?'

'Vet says she'll be fine. We can take the stitches out in a week's time.'

'I'm so glad you're all right, Fupi.' She hugged the little dog to her face, and got licked. 'I'll never let you get into trouble again.'

'Are you well, Lucy?' asked Dad, emerging from the plane, carrying his briefcase.

'Hi, Dad.' She set Fupi down and hugged him.

Diana was the last to get out. 'It's so lovely to be back,' she said. 'I have such happy memories of this place. And it's so warm. Simba can be quite cold at times when the air comes down from Ngorongoro.'

Cold, thought Lucy. You should try Putney in January. She led them over to the cart and introduced Nyati and Mbogo.

'Who's going to ride?' she asked.

'Come on,' said Craig, climbing aboard. 'Are you the driver?'

Lucy grinned.

When they got near the house, Kal came rushing out. 'Lucy, what happened? Where were you? We looked all along the beach, and I was just about to take the dinghy out,' he panted. 'Hi, Mum. Hi, Dad. You okay, Craig? Hi, Diana.'

Lucy was conscious of everyone looking at her. 'I er... came back through the forest.'

'But there's no...'

'Kal, not now!' she hissed. 'I think Mum and Dad would like to ...'

'Lucy!' Faru came hurrying off the veranda. 'Thank goodness.'

'Lucy,' said Mum, 'what *have* you been up to?'

'Er… nothing. I just got lost. I don't know what all the fuss is about.' She climbed down from the cart.

Ellie rushed up and hugged her. Lucy could see she'd been crying.

'Tell us,' said Craig.

Lucy looked down at her feet and scuffed the sand. 'Not now,' she muttered.

✂∂✁

Sleeping arrangements had been sorted out (the children would now be sleeping on camp beds under mosquito nets on the veranda), and Abdul, who still hadn't had the chance to leave, had finished telling them about the discoveries they had made and about Sulman and his travels.

'Goodness, what a lot of excitement you've had,' said Diana.

'Lucy, it's your turn now,' said Faru. 'Tell us what happened.'

Lucy could put it off no longer. 'I got lost – like I said.'

'But how did you get back?'

'I came through the forest.'

Faru stroked his chin. 'There's no way through. It's completely overgrown.'

'There *is* a path,' insisted Lucy. 'Once you get inside, it's really obvious. And it comes out by where the roan antelope are.'

'Lucy, there isn't a path,' said Kal, 'not from the beach, anyway. We went and looked.'

'There is. You can't have looked properly, 'cos that's the way I came.'

Faru shook his head.

'I couldn't find the path at first but then this man showed…' Lucy's hand flew to her mouth.

'A man, what man?' asked Ellie.

Lucy looked down at her hands. 'It was the man I saw on the beach. He showed me where the path was.'

'You let a strange man lead you into the forest?' cried Mum.

'Mum, I was cut off by the tide! It was the only way out.'

'But going off like that.'

'Mum, I could have drowned!'

'What sort of a man?' asked Ellie.

'An old man wearing a turban and a sort of long robe thing.'

'A *kanzu*,' said Faru.

'I don't know what it's called.'

'Did you fall asleep?' asked Kal.

'I might have done.' She looked defiantly at him. 'So what?'

'You were dreaming; that's what.'

Faru nodded. 'Must have been.'

'I wasn't!'

'Huh,' said Kal. 'That, or sunstroke.'

'How do you explain, then, that I came out in the field with the roans? Ask Rashid.'

Kal shrugged.

Craig studied her thoughtfully.

Lucy was close to tears. 'Why won't anyone believe me? I'm *not* making it up.'

'Of course you're not, darling,' said Mum. 'It's just that it's very hot and you've had a rather worrying time.'

'Mum! Can't you…?'

There was a shout. Rashid was at the top of the path that led to the beach, beckoning frantically.

'What on earth?' cried Faru.

Kal jumped up and raced off. 'Let's see,' he called.

Dad and Abdul stayed behind, but the others hurried after him. When they got to the beach, Lucy saw a dugout canoe resting in the shallows. A man was lying face downwards in the bottom; beside him were a facemask, a homemade spear gun, and an underwater torch.

'Is he a fisherman?' asked Lucy, hesitantly.

'Looks like it,' said Faru.

'What's he want a torch for?'

'These people often fish at night – not supposed to, of course. Also, there are caves where rock-cod shelter; they're big fish worth a lot of money. Fisherman sometimes swim into dark caves after them.'

Rashid shook the man's shoulder. There was no response. Rashid turned him over.

The man's face was frozen in a look of utmost terror and his eyes gazed unseeing into Rashid's face.

Rashid recoiled. Mum and Ellie screamed.

'Great heaven's above!' exclaimed Faru.

'Do you know him?' asked Craig.

Faru shook his head.

'He was called Hassan,' murmured Rashid. 'He was not good.'

'He's the man I saw,' said Lucy. She swished the water with her foot, not daring to look at the body. 'He came out of that place over there, where I got cut off.'

'Was he the guy who took you into the forest?' said Kal.

'Of course he wasn't!'

'You seem to have seen an awful lot of strange men.'

'Just shut up, Kal! This man was in his canoe, paddling like he was trying to escape from something. He looked really freaked out.'

'It wasn't something else you imagined?'

'No it wasn't!'

Craig glanced at Lucy then turned to the others. 'We'll pull the canoe onto the beach so it can't drift off. Give me a hand, guys.'

The canoe, which had been made from the hollowed-out

trunk of a tree, was incredibly heavy, and they could drag it no more than a metre or so up the beach.

'That should do for the moment,' said Craig. 'Let's see if there's anything we can learn.' He began examining the body. 'Doesn't look as though he was attacked. No sign of any wounds. Hard to say what killed him.'

'Perhaps he died of fright,' said Lucy, still not daring to look.

'People don't die of fright,' said Kal, 'except in horror films.'

'I reckon this guy might have,' said Craig.

Faru nodded. 'The people along the coast here can be very superstitious. I've certainly heard of such things.'

'*Kwele* – true,' said Rashid.

'We'd better tell the police,' said Craig.

Faru nodded. 'I know the inspector at Watumwani. I'll call him.'

❧

'That one was very bad,' said the inspector, when he and two constables arrived in response to Faru's phone call. 'He has given us much trouble.' He seemed almost relieved to be rid of a problem. The inspector asked a few perfunctory questions, instructed the two constables to wrap the body in an old blanket and put it into the boot of their car; then they left.

'What are we going to do with his things?' asked Lucy, indicating the man's possessions.

'The police should have taken them,' said Faru. 'We'll get them together and I'll take them when I next go by.'

Kal climbed into the canoe. 'Hey, what's this?' He scrabbled in the bottom then showed the others what he'd found. Lying in the palm of his hand was a heavy gold ring with a red stone set in the middle.

'It looks really valuable,' said Lucy.

110

'That man was a thief,' murmured Rashid.

'We should show Abdul,' said Craig. 'See if he can make anything of it.'

They hurried back to the house.

'Good gracious, where did this come from?' cried Abdul, when Kal passed him the ring.

'It was in the bottom of that man's canoe,' said Kal.

Abdul began examining the ring with his magnifying glass. 'Ah! There is an Arabic inscription on the inside.' He screwed up his eyes. 'It says: *Praise be to Allah, Mahmoud Omar.*"'

'Who's Mahmoud Omar?' asked Kal.

'I've no idea,' said Abdul.

'Was it the dead man?'

'Rashid said his name was Hassan,' said Lucy.

'Perhaps he did steal it, then,' said Kal. 'Like Rashid said.'

Abdul pushed his glasses onto his forehead and gazed out to sea. 'Mahmoud and Omar are fairly common names here at the coast,' he said, 'but this ring – this is most unusual and very old.'

CHAPTER 13

Rock-cod

THE SLAVE CAVE

Lucy was woken next morning by someone shaking her.

'I'm going to the beach, Lucy,' whispered Kal. 'You coming?'

She peered through the mosquito net and could just make out his shape in the darkness.

'Kal, it's still dark. That's crazy!'

Ellie gave a snore and muttered something in her sleep.

'It'll be light in about twenty minutes,' he whispered. 'I want to check that place where the Sinawe River comes out.'

'Kal, are you mad?'

'Shh. It's probably the only chance we'll get. There's a really low tide this morning.'

'But that man in the canoe, he saw something or…'

'So – we go and find what it was.'

'And get scared witless?'

'No way. Remember, Faru said the guys here are really superstitious. I bet there's a simple explanation. I'm going to find it.'

Lucy stared at Kal for a moment then lay down again. 'You go on your own and don't blame me if you get freaked out.'

'I'm not scared that easily.'

'Kal, you've no idea what you'll find.'

'That's why I'm going.'

Fupi, who had been sleeping at the foot of Lucy's bed, was awake and looking eagerly between the two of them.

Lucy sighed and sat up. 'I suppose someone has to look after you,' she muttered.

'Thanks. We'll be fine, Lucy. We'll take flippers and things, and torches in case there's a cave or something like Faru said. I'll meet you at the top of the path to the beach. Don't wake the others.'

Five minutes later, they were heading along the beach to the place where the Sinawe River emerged from the forest. Fupi trotted between them looking enquiringly from one to the other. The pinkish glow in the sky showed that dawn wasn't far away but when they reached the creek, everything was in deep shadow. They could hear gurgling and sloshing sounds of water among the rocks.

'Looks really spooky,' said Lucy.

'We'll have to wait for the sun to come up,' said Kal. He peered at the dark water in the channel below them. 'The water's quite low but I think the tide's still going out. That means there won't be any sharks,' he added with a grin.

Lucy pursed her lips but didn't mention what she had seen the previous day when the tide was in. Instead, she said: 'That's where the man in the canoe came from.' She pointed. 'From round that corner.'

'Right.'

They sat with their feet dangling over the edge of the creek and waited for the sun. There was no wind to rustle the trees and the only sound was that of the restless water.

'It's not quite so scary when you get used to it,' said Lucy.

'It's cool,' said Kal.

Fupi looked at the two of them and wagged her tail.

In almost no time, the rim of the sun appeared and birds began to sing as light flooded across the forest and the beach. A flurry of breeze skittered across the water making the sunlight shimmer on the ripples.

'It was so weird seeing that old man,' said Lucy. 'He was standing just there – where Fupi's sniffing.'

'Yeah.'

'Kal, I don't mind your not believing me.'

Kal studied his sister for a moment. 'I'm going to try the river,' he said, and slithered down the bank into the water, which was only waist deep. 'It's almost stopped flowing. I don't reckon we'll need the flippers.' He waded off round the corner.

'Wait for me,' called Lucy. She slid into the water then reached out for Fupi. The little dog didn't look very happy but Lucy knew she wouldn't want to be left behind.

Lucy followed Kal upstream. When she reached him, he was peering into an opening in the rock face.

'Looks like the entrance to a cave or something,' he said, 'but see, it's only partly exposed, even at a really low tide. Mostly, it would be hidden underwater all the time.'

'Kal, I'm not sure this is a good idea. It looks really dangerous.'

'Hang on, I'll go back and get the torches.'

While Kal was gone, Lucy studied the dark opening. One or two crabs crawled around on the rock face outside. Inside was black and sinister, and she could hear the menacing murmur of sloshing water.

Kal returned.

'I don't think it's safe,' said Lucy. 'We should go back.'

'Let's see.' Kal waded across to the entrance, ducked his head down and disappeared.

Lucy chewed her lip as she watched and waited.

Kal reappeared. 'It's cool,' he said. 'It's massive and there are no ghosts.'

'Don't say that!'

'Come on.' He passed her one of the torches and headed back to the cave.

Lucy followed. It was a struggle trying to keep Fupi and the torch out of the water and not bang her head on the roof of the entrance, but when she was inside, the ground led upwards into a large cave and she could put Fupi down. It smelled strongly of sea and seaweed, and she could hear water dripping and a strange rustling sound.

'Kal, what's that noise?' Her trembling voice echoed eerily off the walls. 'That funny sort of rustling – listen.'

'There!' Kal shone his torch.

It took Lucy's eyes a moment to adjust to the dim light. 'Crabs! There's millions of crabs! Kal, I don't like this.'

The crabs were everywhere – some were even on the roof of the cave – the light reflecting back from their red eyes.

'And what's that?' cried Lucy, as Kal's torch picked up a dark shape high up in the far wall.

'Dunno. Looks like some sort of hole.'

'We shouldn't have come, Kal. It's horrible in here.'

'We've got to have a look round. See if we can find out what freaked that guy.'

'But it was high tide; how would he get in?' she asked. 'We had enough difficulty at low tide.'

'He could dive down. Remember, these guys are good swimmers – and he had a torch with him.'

'You think he came looking for those… those rock-cod like Faru said?'

'Could be. I guess they might swim in here at high tide.' Kal shone his torch around and began to investigate further.

Lucy glanced across towards the entrance; light was seeping into the cave but it hardly penetrated and it gave a sinister quality to the water, which was washing gently in and out with that menacing murmuring. 'Kal, we mustn't stay long.'

'Hey, Lucy, come and see this,' called Kal, who was examining something on the cave wall.

As she scrambled over the slippery floor to join him, the crabs scurried away across the rocks.

Fupi whined and kept close on her heels.

Lucy peered where Kal was shining his torch. 'What is it, and what's that brownish stain?'

'I reckon there's been an iron peg or something hammered into the rock but it's all rusted away; that's what the stain is.' He shone his torch around. 'Look, there's another. And there's one that hasn't... it's an iron ring.'

Lucy's hand flew to her mouth. 'Kal, you know what these are?'

'I guess it could be where they tied up boats or something.'

'Don't be daft. There's no way they'd get boats in here.'

'What then?'

'Kal, it's where they chained up slaves! Don't you remember what Abdul was saying, how the slaves were chained in caves that linked to the sea.'

'You reckon this is one of those caves?'

'It's got to be. It's just like Abdul described.'

Fupi gave a low growl.

Lucy bent down and picked her up. 'It's all right, Fupi, I know it's scary but it's quite safe. I'll take care of...' She was about to put the little dog down, when she noticed a movement deep inside the cave. The hairs on the back of her neck began to prickle. She shone the torch but all she could see were crabs scuttling away from the light and shadows that made weird shapes as she moved the torch around. Then her breath caught in her throat. She felt Fupi trembling. Someone was in the cave with

116

them! Her heart was pounding. She tried to speak but no sound came out. It was the man – the one who had led her through the forest! He smiled and gave a slight bow. She looked across at Kal who had moved off to examine another iron ring. Surely he'd seen the man. She looked back. The man was gone.

Lucy's voice recovered. 'Wait!' she called.

'Wait?' called Kal. 'What do you mean – wait?'

'Kal, it was him. That man was here!'

'Yeah, right.' Kal flashed his torch around the cave. Strange shapes danced off the wall. 'Look,' he said, 'there's a bat, and there's a dinosaur and that's a space ship.'

'All right, don't believe me. Just look after Fupi.' She stumbled across to Kal and placed the little dog in his arms. Fupi licked his face.

'Yuk!'

'It's only a bit of lick.'

'I know that but she also licks other places,' grumbled Kal.

'Don't make such a fuss,' said Lucy. She made her way over to where she had seen the man and shone her torch into the depths of the cave. Her heart was pounding again.

'Kal!' she screamed. 'Quick!'

Kal hurried across. He gave a sudden intake of breath as he saw the bleached skeleton lying at the back of the cave above the high water mark.

'And look, the remains of a chain!'

'The poor guy was chained up and left.'

'What a horrible way to die.' Lucy screwed up her eyes.

Kal looked more closely at the skeleton. 'There's something wrong,' he muttered.

'You're telling me!'

'No, it's something…'

'Kal, the tide's coming in!' She grabbed his arm.

They stumbled towards the entrance, Fupi running ahead

whining. The water swirled and gurgled angrily as it washed into the cave.

Lucy shone her torch for a last look back. Was that shape a dinosaur? Or was it an old man in a turban and *kanzu*, bowing?

Fupi barked.

Lucy picked her up.

'It's really shifting!' cried Kal. He stuffed the torch into the waistband of his shorts and grabbed Lucy's wrist, dragging her forward against the surging water.

'We're not going to make it,' she wailed.

'Shut up!'

Lucy could feel the tide trying to sweep them back into the cave. Fupi whimpered as Lucy gripped her under her arm.

Kal swore as he fought against the relentless current.

Lucy banged her head on the rock above and her feet slipped from under her. Kal's hand locked on her wrist and he pulled her out.

Then they were clear.

'Thanks for hanging on,' gasped Lucy, wiping her face.

Fupi sneezed, trying to get the water out of her nose.

'It's all right, Fupi,' said Lucy, 'we're safe now.'

They looked back. The cave entrance was under water. They glanced at each other, said nothing, and waded back to where they'd left their things.

'You guys were cutting things a bit fine,' said a voice.

'Craig!' cried Lucy. She reached out a hand and Craig pulled her up the bank out of the water.

'Where have you been?'

'We've er… we've been exploring.'

'I see.'

'How did you know where we were?'

Craig pointed at the damp sand. 'It didn't exactly need a Matata to follow those tracks.'

Lucy grinned. 'We'll walk backwards next time. That'll trick you.'

As they headed along the beach, Lucy and Kal told Craig everything that had happened.

'Craig, do you think that skeleton could have been one of the slaves Abdul was telling us about?' said Lucy.

'I guess so.'

'I don't think we should tell the others,' she said. 'You know how worried Mum might get.'

Craig nodded. 'Okay – for the moment, anyway. But we'll have to inform the police at some stage.'

They made their way up the path.

'Ah, there you are,' called Faru, who was standing at the top of the veranda steps. 'Just in time for a quick breakfast then we'll be off.'

'Where are we going?' asked Lucy.

'You'll see,' said Faru, a twinkle in his eye.

CHAPTER 14

Roan antelope

BULLET AND ARROW

Lucy and Kal climbed the steps to the veranda and joined the others at breakfast.

'*Jambo*, Lucy. *Jambo*, Kal,' said a voice, and there was Martha coming through, carrying a bowl of fruit.

'Martha!' cried Lucy. 'You've come.'

Martha smiled. 'We came this morning. Now I am helping Hannah. Samson and Matata have gone in the truck.'

'Here they are now,' said Faru, as a large truck like a horsebox came into view moving slowly along the sandy track that led to the house. Samson was at the wheel with Matata sitting beside him. Lucy waved and they waved back. Then the truck disappeared behind the house.

As soon as she had finished breakfast, Lucy ran to find the truck. She stopped and stared. Samson and Rashid were leading two horses out of the back. Fupi, who had followed Lucy, eyed them warily.

'Well done, you fellows,' said Faru, as he came to join her.

'Faru, what's happening?' said Lucy.

'For you and Ellie, my dear.'

Lucy's jaw dropped. Me and my big mouth. I should never have said we could ride. Hacking in Richmond Park was one thing, riding these… these racehorses in the African bush would be something else.

Craig, Ellie and Kal arrived to see what was going on.

'What are the horses for?' asked Ellie.

'We're riding them when we help round up the roans,' said Lucy airily.

'What!'

'Faru says they're really very quiet.' Faru hadn't actually said that but Lucy was sure he would.

They watched the horses skittering around, with Samson holding the ropes attached to their head collars, and trying to calm them. Craig went to help.

'They're called Risasi and Mshale,' said Faru.

'Meaning what?' asked Lucy.

Now Ellie looked really nervous. 'Their names mean Bullet and Arrow.'

'Good names for nice quiet nags,' said Kal.

Faru chuckled. 'Ex polo ponies; they're a bit lively after their journey.'

'But I thought you said…'

Lucy hastily interrupted Ellie. 'Where do you keep them?' she asked.

'They stay inland on a friend's farm, away from the tsetse,' said Faru.

'The what?'

'Tsetse flies; they transmit a disease called sleeping sickness. Horses are very susceptible.'

'What about people?'

Faru shook his head. 'Plenty of tsetse here but they don't carry human sleeping sickness – only the animal form.'

'Will the horses be all right?'

'We spray them before they go out, to kill any flies which land on them,' said Faru. 'Here's Rashid now.'

Rashid emerged from a shed carrying a stirrup pump and a bucket containing a milky-looking liquid. Then, while he operated the pump, Faru sprayed the animals all over. They were obviously used to it because they stood quite still. Lucy began to feel reassured.

When Faru had finished, he and Samson led the horses into the shade and tied them to posts.

Fupi sniffed them suspiciously then ran back to the house, clearly wanting no further part in the day's proceedings.

'Right, girls, into jeans,' said Craig. 'We'll set off in an hour.'

'I'm not sure I want to...' began Ellie.

'Nonsense,' said Faru. 'Like riding donkeys on the beach in your country.'

'I've never ridden a donkey.'

'Or a polo pony,' murmured Lucy.

'You coming with us, Kal?' asked Craig.

Kal looked uncertain. 'I think Faru said something about a...'

'Gracious!' cried Faru. 'I nearly forgot.' He hurried into the shed, and they could hear what sounded like a motorbike starting up. A few minutes later, he emerged at the seat of a bright blue Yamaha Banshee 350 cc twin-cylinder quad bike. He switched off the engine.

'That is mean,' breathed Kal, fondly running his hands over the controls. 'Can I try it?'

'Go ahead,' said Faru.

Kal looked round the others and grinned then climbed onto the seat and started the engine. It gave a gentle puttering sound.

Kal eased open the throttle and the bike emitted a deeper growl suggesting hidden power. The horses shifted uneasily. Kal licked dry lips. 'Awesome.'

'Ever ridden one before?' asked Faru.

Kal shook his head.

'Quite straightforward.'

Five minutes later, Kal went for a practice run. He could feel the power throbbing through the handlebars. He opened the throttle. The bike leapt forward almost unseating him. Wicked! He eased off the throttle and drove back to the others.

Matata's eyes were popping out of his head.

'Can Mat ride with me?' asked Kal. ' There's enough room.'

Faru considered for a moment then when back into the shed. 'Provided you wear these.' He came out holding two crash helmets.

An hour later, they set off. Craig and Faru led in Faru's elderly Land Rover, Samson and Rashid travelling with them. The girls came next on the horses, and Kal and Matata brought up the rear.

At first, the horses wanted to jogtrot sideways. If the girls turned their heads to the front, they started to canter although they were travelling at little more than walking pace. But the girls soon remembered their riding lessons: sit firmly in the saddle, grip with the knees, keep hands low, and control the reins from the wrists. As soon as the horses realised the girls knew what they were doing they settled down.

They reached the paddock where Lucy had previously seen the roans, and where the stockade was, but there were no antelope. Lucy looked to see where the path came out of the forest. There was no sign.

'I didn't imagine it,' she murmured. 'I know I didn't.'

Faru led the group along a track through the trees at the end of the paddock. After about fifty metres, the trees opened out into a much larger area of grass, bushes and trees. The roans were at the far end.

Craig stopped in the shade, the girls got down from their horses, Kal switched off the quad bike and everyone gathered round Faru.

'There's about thirty of them,' he said, pointing, 'thirty two to be precise, plus a few calves.' He turned to Craig. 'You're the expert, what do we do?'

Craig studied the animals through his binoculars. 'We need to take out a nucleus group,' he murmured, 'one male and half a dozen or so females. The difficulty will be separating them.'

'There are four bulls,' said Faru. 'Getting one of those fellows out will be the problem.'

Craig nodded.

'Chuki's the one to watch.'

'Which one's Chuki?' asked Lucy.

Faru pointed. 'That one over there on his own.'

Craig lowered his binoculars. 'Right, guys, this is how we play it: we'll drive the whole herd back through the trees; there's no way we can split them up where they are – too much space. Then we'll corral them in the *boma* – the stockade – there, and sort them out that way.'

'Sounds pretty straightforward,' said Kal.

Craig grinned. 'That's what worries me.' He turned to the girls. 'Lucy and Ellie, ride down this side of the herd then walk quietly back behind them. The horses won't bother them. Kal, you and Matata go round the other side, but keep well clear otherwise the quad bike could spook them. Your job is to round up any stragglers or animals that try to break back.'

'Copy that,' said Kal.

Craig turned to Samson and Rashid. 'You know what to do?'
They nodded and set off back through the trees.

'Faru and I will be in the Land Rover directing operations from that side,' said Craig, pointing. 'Make sure you guys watch us so that we can signal to you. Any questions?'

They all shook their heads.

'Let's give it a go,' said Craig. He helped Lucy and Ellie back into their saddles. 'Will you be all right?'

'I hope so.' Lucy smiled nervously.

'You'll be fine; just don't rush things – we've got all day. Good luck.'

The girls set off at a gentle trot.

'You guys, okay?' asked Craig, turning to the two boys.

'Sure,' said Kal.

'No heroics, now, but you may have to move fast. If one of the roans breaks back, the rest will try and follow.'

'No sweat,' said Kal. He climbed onto the quad bike and started the engine. Matata climbed on behind him.

'*Shika sana* – hold tight,' called Craig.

Matata grinned and put his arms round Kal's waist.

Lucy looked across at Ellie. 'Isn't this great?'

'Brilliant,' cried Ellie, who had now lost her worried expression. 'Richmond Park will seem very tame after this.'

They let the horses canter gently down beside the herd. The roans looked up but took very little notice, and soon resumed their grazing.

Lucy pointed. 'That bull's joined the group, the one that Faru said we had to watch.'

'He's called Chuki,' said Ellie. 'Do you know what that means?'

125

'No.'

'It means bad-tempered or stroppy.'

'I don't like the sound of that.'

They slowed to a trot and moved the horses closer to the herd. Chuki looked annoyed at being disturbed and one or two of the other animals snorted. Lucy and Ellie slowed to a walk.

'We shouldn't talk any more,' whispered Lucy.

Ellie nodded.

They were now behind the herd, which had closed up into a more compact group. Lucy watched Kal and Matata moving down the far side. Some of the roans seemed uneasy and moved away from the sound of the quad bike.

Lucy and Ellie eased the herd forward, Lucy concentrating on the left side, and Ellie on the right. If any animals started to wander off, one of the girls would trot across and urge them back in.

Suddenly, Chuki turned and bolted. Lucy dug in her heels. Risasi shot forward and just managed to cut off Chuki's escape. He stopped, snorted and then turned back.

'Well done,' said Lucy, patting the horse's neck. 'Bullet's a jolly good name for you.' The horse was panting with the sudden exertion. 'We can't afford to relax, Risasi,' she murmured.

The rest of the herd had seen what had happened and were getting restless. Lucy and Ellie now had to work harder to keep them together, cantering backwards and forwards at the rear. But the animals – Chuki in particular – were reluctant to leave their current grazing. This time he put his head down and made a determined run. Lucy was too late. He broke free and was just about to head back to the open, when there was a roar from the quad bike and Kal raced across. Chuki stood snorting for a moment and lowered his head, the wicked-looking horns pointing menacingly towards the quad bike. Kal remained stationary and watchful. He revved the engine. Chuki snorted and tossed his head, then turned and trotted back to the rest of the herd.

'Well done, Kal,' called Craig. 'Drop back a bit, everyone. Let them find their own way.'

One or two of the animals started to wander along the track through the trees. Craig signalled the children to close up, and the rest of the herd followed with no further trouble.

'That was the easy bit,' said Craig.

CHAPTER 15

Ruined house

THE BAD-TEMPERED ANTELOPE

The children stared in amazement: Rashid and Samson had just finished enclosing a large area of the paddock in a wall of green fabric that linked up to the high wooden fence of the *boma*.

'The roans don't realise that the walls of the corral aren't solid,' said Craig. 'The idea is that we gradually reduce its size by moving the walls inwards, and that will funnel the roans into the *boma* – the stockade. We hope,' he added with a grin.

While the boys waited with Faru and the Land Rover outside the corral, Craig and Samson sealed off the back, leaving the girls on their horses inside with the roans.

Chuki wasn't settling. He was trotting along the green wall snorting and looking for a gap. This made the other animals restless. Any minute now he might discover that the wall was not solid and all their careful preparations would have been in vain. Lucy and Ellie tried to push him back into the herd but he ignored the horses and continued his restlessness.

'We'll have to dart him,' called Craig. 'I'll get the gear. You girls, back off, before he loses it.'

Lucy and Ellie drew back and watched. Chuki glared at them, snorted and stamped a front foot. Then with no warning, he charged straight at Risasi, who leapt to the side, unseating Lucy. She landed on the ground with a thump, all the air knocked out of her body. Risasi ran off, stopped and looked back. Lucy lay on the ground, not moving, with Chuki standing about ten paces away looking at her and pawing the ground. He started to walk towards her on stiff legs then he lowered his head.

'No!' screamed Ellie.

'*Acha*!' yelled a voice. Matata had ducked under the wall and was running at Chuki, shouting.

Chuki stopped and transferred his attention from the senseless Lucy to Matata, who was leaping up and down waving his arms. Chuki snorted and shook his head.

Craig had prepared the darting equipment, and hearing the shouting, rushed back from the Land Rover, scrambled under the wall and ran towards Lucy. For a moment, Chuki was distracted. Matata gave another great shout. Chuki turned and charged him. Craig dashed forward, picked up Lucy and ran with her to safety.

Chuki was now on Matata's heels. He lowered his head with those wicked horns pointing forward and closed on Matata. Chuki tossed his head, and as the horns came raking back, Matata dodged, rolled to the side and was back on his feet in an instant, grinning. Chuki whirled round and came again. Again, Matata dodged and rolled away.

Chuki stopped. He was panting heavily.

Matata turned and ran.

Chuki lowered his head and came in once more. Just as those fearsome horns came sweeping up, Matata leapt up onto the high fence surrounding the *boma* and scrambled out of harm's way. He was still grinning. No one else was.

Lucy began to stir.

'Ellie!' shouted Craig. 'Give me your horse and look after Lucy.'

Ellie jumped down, and Craig leapt into the saddle not bothering to fit his feet in the stirrups. He gathered the reins in one hand, pulled a darting pistol from the holster on his belt and cantered towards Chuki.

The roan looked up and charged.

Craig held the trembling Mshale steady. At the last minute, he threw the reins across the horse's neck, kicked hard, and Mshale spun round with the agility he had learned on the polo field. As Chuki tore past, almost brushing the horse's flank, Craig fired the pistol and the tranquillizer dart lodged in the roan's backside.

Chuki whirled round, enraged by the sting of the dart, and charged again.

Craig dug in his heels and Mshale leapt forward.

Chuki was closing on him.

Craig did another polo turn.

Chuki couldn't stop. The green wall ripped as he ran into it. He paused momentarily seeing the thick forest ahead, jumped the wire fence, crashed through the undergrowth just beside the tree with the great swollen trunk, and was gone – still with the dart lodged in his backside, its red tuft clearly visible.

'Matata,' shouted Craig, '*fanya haraka, mfuata* – quick, follow him!'

But Matata was already on his way. He raced across the paddock, leapt the fence and disappeared through the gap in the bushes made by Chuki.

'Faru, Rashid, Samson,' shouted Craig, 'stay here and make sure the others don't escape. Kal, get the Landy and follow me.'

Kal ran to the Land Rover, started the engine and drove across to where Craig was smashing at the wire fence with a large branch.

'Force your way in, Kal,' called Craig. 'Low ratio.'

Kal eased the Land Rover forward. The wire snapped and sprang back, and the bushes began to give way. 'Look out!' he yelled.

A large green snake slithered across the bonnet, shot across Craig's feet and disappeared back into the bush.

'What was that?' cried Kal.

'Green mamba,' said Craig. 'One of the worst.'

Kal wiped a hand across his face and gulped.

'Just go slowly,' said Craig, 'in case there're any more.'

The thick vegetation was no match for the relentless power of the vehicle, and once Kal had forced a way through the outer bushes, the inner forest opened out into a woodland of shading trees. But there was no sign of Matata or Chuki.

'They can't be too far away,' said Craig, 'that *dawa* takes about ten minutes to work.' He looked at his watch. 'Should just about be...'

There was a cry. Matata came racing back through the trees, waving his arms, shouting and looking terrified.

'*Namna gani* – what is it?' cried Craig, bundling Matata into the vehicle.

'Which way – *wapi*?' yelled Kal.

Matata pointed, still shouting incoherently.

'What's the matter?' cried Kal, setting off through the trees as fast as he dared.

'Don't know. I think he saw something,' cried Craig. 'Right a bit, Kal, into that clearing.'

Kal threaded the vehicle between the trees.

Matata grabbed Craig's arm and pointed. A small reddish brown animal with a pointed nose was staring towards the vehicle.

'Elephant-shrew,' said Craig.

Matata was trembling.

'Surely *that's* not bugging him,' muttered Kal, switching off the engine.

The animal disappeared into some bushes.

'Hang on,' said Craig. He jumped out of the Land Rover, and ran after the elephant-shrew.

Matata kept giving convulsive shudders despite Kal's efforts to reassure him.

Craig came running back. 'Chuki's in there flat out.'

'What are we going to do?'

'I'll take Matata and get the sledge. Kal, you wait here to guide me back in.'

'Sure.' Kal jumped down from the driving seat. 'But don't expect me to look after Chuki.'

'He'll be fine. I've removed the dart.' Craig started the Land Rover. 'Will you be okay?'

'Yeah. I'll have a look round, see if I can work out what freaked Mat.'

'Won't be long,' called Craig, setting off back through the trees.

Kal watched the vehicle until it was out of sight then wandered over to the bushes. Chuki lay on his side breathing heavily, but Craig had raised his head by propping a log underneath. All around, the branches had been smashed where Chuki had staggered about before collapsing. Kal studied the animal. He really was magnificent: those tremendous neck muscles; that beautiful colouring; and those horns – he wouldn't want to mess with this guy. Without Lucy watching him, Kal was quite happy to take an interest in something not mechanical.

He felt a sudden chill and the hairs on the back of his neck rose. He kept very still.

He was being watched.

He held his breath and slowly turned his head.

That animal was there – that one with the pointy nose. It was looking straight at him. He breathed out. A poxy elephant-shrew! But he still felt uneasy.

The animal gave a squeak and scampered off. Kal watched it disappear into a thicket on the far side of the clearing. 'Bit odd,' he murmured, 'but it doesn't exactly freak me out. And there's no way Mat would have... What's that? Looks like a...' He walked slowly towards the thicket and saw it was an old building – or rather, the ruin of an old building. It was covered in creepers. There was no roof and part of one wall had collapsed. Kal didn't dare go too close for fear of snakes. An old wooden door, partly rotted, which was carved rather like Faru's Lamu chest, leaned off rusted hinges. Beyond it, Kal saw a doorway leading to black nothingness.

It could be the old Arab place that Faru mentioned. His thoughts were cut short by the sound of the Land Rover returning. He ran to the middle of the clearing and waved. Craig turned the vehicle towards him and Kal saw a large wooden sledge being towed behind.

Craig had Samson with him, but no Matata.

'Is Mat okay?' asked Kal, as Craig drew up.

'I think so, but there's no way he's coming back,' said Craig.

'He has been badly frightened,' said Samson. 'He says he saw a house and an old man who vanished.'

'There's a ruined house over there,' said Kal pointing, 'but there's no old man – only that guy.' He indicated the elephant-shrew. 'He keeps popping up.'

'We'll come and check it out later,' said Craig. 'Let's get Chuki sorted first.'

Between them they rolled the now-peaceful antelope onto the sledge. Craig put a sack over its head, and another full of straw underneath to keep the head raised.

'You drive, Kal,' said Craig. 'Samson and I'll ride on the sledge to hold Chuki steady.'

⁓⊙⋐⌐

The inside of the truck had been fitted out with a number of solid-walled pens, all of which were covered in heavily-padded canvas. Matata was inside spreading a thick layer of straw on the floor. Kal pulled up beside the open back of the truck.

'How's it going?' he called to Matata.

Matata grinned. 'Now, very fine. There, very bad.'

Kal jumped down from the Land Rover. 'Tell me later.'

The two of them went to the back of the vehicle to help Samson unhitch the sledge. Craig, meanwhile, had pulled out the cable from a winch that was mounted inside the truck. He hooked the cable to the sledge and started the motor. Gradually, the sledge was drawn up the tailgate and into the truck, with Chuki and Matata – grinning like mad – riding with it. Craig stopped the motor and they rolled Chuki onto the straw. Matata dragged out the empty sledge and Craig closed off various partitions so that Chuki was now contained in a small pen that he would have to himself until he got to Simba.

'How are you getting on?' called a shaky voice.

'You okay, now, Lucy?' asked Craig.

She gave a watery grin. 'I've got a massive bruise on my bum, but otherwise all right.'

'Good on you.'

'I told you bad things happen in threes,' she said. 'That was the third.'

'Thank goodness for that,' said Kal. 'I can now sleep soundly.'

Lucy ignored him. 'Can I help?' she asked.

'Sure,' said Craig. 'Just in time.' He went back to the Land Rover and returned carrying a syringe and a bottle. He drew some

134

yellowish liquid into the syringe and handed it to Lucy. 'There you go; that's the antidote. Come.' He led her into the pen where Chuki was lying peacefully. 'Stab the needle in quickly,' he said.

'Here?' Lucy pointed to the animal's rear.

Craig nodded.

Lucy stabbed. Nothing happened.

'Harder,' said Craig.

Lucy stabbed again. The needle slid through the skin and into the thick muscle.

'Good,' said Craig. 'Now gently pull the plunger back to check you're not in a blood vessel.'

Lucy eased back the plunger but nothing happened. She looked questioningly at Craig.

'That's fine, Lucy. See, no blood so you're not in the wrong place. Go ahead and inject.'

She pressed the plunger. 'I hope you now have a sore bum as well, Chuki,' she said with a grin, handing the syringe back to Craig.

'Quick!' Craig whipped the sack off Chuki's head, pulled Lucy out of the pen, and bolted the door. 'See here.' He indicated a spy hole in the wall.

Lucy peered through. 'Chuki's already getting up!'

Craig nodded. 'That antidote works very quickly.'

⤳⥈⤶

While Chuki was being rescued, Faru and Rashid had managed to sort out the other roans and selected six females, including two with calves, and put them in a smaller pen within the *boma*. The remaining animals had been released.

'Do you think Chuki will cause trouble at Simba?' asked Lucy, as she and the others leaned over the fence looking at the penned animals.

Craig shook his head. 'He'll be the only bull and he'll just have the females for company.'

'Poor guy,' muttered Kal. 'Bet they sort him out.'

Faru chuckled.

They watched as Samson, Matata and Rashid rigged up a large tarpaulin to provide some shade in the corner of the pen, then Matata filled up the water trough.

Craig called out to him: '*Kazi yako, sasa* – they're your responsibility now.'

Matata grinned and waved.

'Mat is so cool,' said Kal. 'He just wasn't afraid of Chuki.'

'That's what comes of spending his life in the bush,' said Craig. 'He understands the animals far better than I ever will.'

'But something freaked him out in the forest,' added Kal.

Craig nodded and frowned. 'I know. I wonder what it could have been.'

'Did you find the path?' asked Lucy.

'What path?' said Kal.

'The one I was telling you about, where I came out of the forest.'

Kal held his sister's eyes. 'Lucy, there is no path.'

CHAPTER 16

Arab dhow

A NEW ARRIVAL

First thing next morning, Lucy went with Craig to see the roans. They climbed onto the wall of the *boma* and looked in. Matata was already there giving the animals some hay and talking quietly to them.

'Where are the horses?' asked Lucy.

'Samson took them back yesterday evening,' said Craig. 'Chuki had to go along for the ride.'

'Wonder what they said to each other,' mused Lucy. 'Bet it was a bit rude.'

Matata waved and called to them, indicating the far corner of the *boma*.

Lucy looked where he was pointing and gasped. 'A baby calf!'

'*Dume*,' called Matata.

'It's a male – born in the night,' said Craig. 'Let's hope it's not related to Chuki, then we can avoid the risk of inbreeding when the herd gets established.'

'That's fantastic!' cried Lucy. 'What's Swahili for "luck"?'

'*Bahati* – why?'

'We should call the new calf, Bahati.'

Craig smiled. 'Good name. Bahati, it is.'

Samson joined them as they watched the animals.

'Are they going to Simba today?' asked Lucy.

Samson nodded. 'It's a long drive – about six to eight hours.'

'Let's move it, then,' said Craig. 'You ready for more veterinary work, Lucy?'

'Y-e-s,' she said cautiously.

A short while later, she and Craig were kneeling outside the *boma* beside the roan with the newborn calf. There were plenty of gaps in the fence, and although the mother was aware of their presence, she wasn't too worried. This time Craig had mounted the darting syringe on the end of a pole. Lucy slid this through the fence and stabbed it into the mother, who barely flinched. Craig nodded his approval. They waited. Finally, the roan's head started to droop and she slumped sideways onto the ground.

Craig and Lucy scrambled over the fence to join Matata and Samson. Between them, they carried the mother and calf into the truck, which Samson had made ready. They adjusted the internal partitions so that the mother and baby had their own pen, then Lucy, under Craig's watchful eye, administered the antidote. They could hear Chuki snorting his disapproval in the adjacent pen.

The other roans in the *boma* had watched proceedings with interest. Matata now called to them. Gradually they responded to his voice and walked towards the truck. They needed a bit of coaxing from Craig and Samson to get them up the ramp but finally they were all loaded.

Lucy and Craig leaned over the partition and looked at the new mother who was licking her baby, which was now suckling. 'Why did we have to dart her?' Lucy asked.

'With her newborn calf, she would be very protective and could be dangerous; not like Chuki – she's that much smaller – but we couldn't afford to take any chances.'

'What will happen to them when they arrive?'

'There's a big fenced paddock we'll put them in for a start,' said Craig, 'then we'll release them into the ranch once they've settled.'

An hour later, Lucy waved goodbye to Samson, Martha and Matata. 'Say hi to Caspar and Carmen, and Mondo and all the other animals,' she called. She was sad to see them go but Matata had the roans to look after and Samson needed to keep an eye on the ranch while Craig was away.

'And I have to look after these men,' Martha said, smiling. 'They don't eat properly if I am not there.'

Lucy laughed, then watched and waved until they were out of sight. She turned and set off back to the house for breakfast. With all the excitement, she had forgotten how stiff and bruised she felt after yesterday's tumble. Now the pain came flooding back.

⁂

'What's the matter with you?' asked Kal, as Lucy hobbled up the steps onto the veranda. 'You're walking like the butler from some Dracula movie.'

'So would you,' she snapped, 'if your bum was as bruised.' She eased herself into a chair and glared at Kal.

'Are you sure you're all right, darling?' asked Mum.

'Provided people don't keep making grotty remarks.' She helped herself to some pineapple and looked defiantly round the table.

'Backs can be nasty things,' said Faru. 'I remember when I...'
He caught sight of Lucy's venomous scowl. 'I er... was about to
say that swimming's the thing – eases the muscles, as it were.'

Lucy didn't respond but helped herself to another piece of
pineapple.

The children spent the rest of the morning snorkelling in the
warm clear sea of the marine reserve and lazing in the glass-
bottomed dinghy as it drifted over the coral. Lucy insisted on
taking Fupi, who, once she had become used to the motion of
the dinghy, stood with her front paws on the prow peering at the
fascinating creatures slipping past beneath them. She only fell in
once at the excitement of seeing a shoal of cuttlefish shoot by.
After that she was more wary and made no attempt to join Lucy
when she was snorkelling.

Faru had given Lucy some laminated cards on which were
pictures of the reef fishes. Now, as she floated in the shallow sea
peering through her face mask and checking the cards, she began
to recognise butterflyfish poking their sharp noses into the
branches of coral; clownfish sheltering amongst the tentacles of
sea anemones, impervious to their sting; parrotfish rasping the
coral with their horny mouths (she could even hear the sound);
lion or scorpionfish waving their poisonous-spined fins; surgeon-
fish with sharp scalpels by their tails; and many more: coachmen,
Moorish idols, cleaner wrasse, cardinalfish, trigger-fish, angel-
fish, groupers, snappers – the variety seemed endless. She forgot
all sense of time and place within this marine wonderland of
which she was a part.

She was vaguely aware of someone calling. She lifted her
head and saw Kal beckoning. 'Come and see this, Lucy.'

She kicked her flippers, paddled swiftly across and peered

through her facemask. 'I can't see anything. It's just seaweed.'

'It's really well camouflaged,' said Kal. 'Watch.' He dived down with his arm outstretched and nearly touched the lump on the sea bed, before it shot off in a cloud of ink.

'An octopus!' cried Lucy.

Faru was right; most of the stiffness in her back had now gone.

They finished snorkelling and were on their way back from the beach, Fupi trotting ahead and looking very pleased with herself, when a car drew up by the house and the driver got out.

'Hello, Abdul,' shouted Lucy.

'Some good news,' he called, waving his briefcase.

'We've also got some news,' said Kal, as they greeted him.

'Ah ha!'

'We've found an old building in the forest which could be that Arab place you told us about.'

'How exciting. You must show me.'

The four of them hurried onto the veranda and joined the others who were having drinks and chatting.

'Abdul has some good news,' said Ellie.

'Tell us,' said Faru.

'Yes, yes,' said Abdul, 'but I want to see this ruined house in the forest – most exciting. When can we go?'

'Kal and I will show you,' said Craig, 'but first your news.'

'Right.' Abdul put his briefcase on the table, pulled out an old book and opened it at a page he had marked with a slip of paper.

'Does anyone know who that might be?' he asked.

They looked at the illustration and all but Lucy shook their heads.

'Lucy, do you know?' asked Abdul.

'No,' she whispered. She turned away from the others so they couldn't see her face. It was the old man who had led her through the forest.

Craig watched her but said nothing.

'Who is it, Abdul?' asked Faru.

Abdul held up the book so that they could see its title.

'*A History Of The Slave Trade In East Africa*,' read Ellie.

'That's it,' said Abdul. 'This picture shows an old woodcut print of a man called Mahmoud Omar.'

'The name on the ring!' cried Ellie.

'Precisely.'

'A slave trader?'

'No.'

'Abdul, you've got to tell us,' said Ellie.

'Hang on a moment,' said Craig. He disappeared inside the house, returning a few moments later with the ring, which he placed on the table.

Ellie picked it up then peered at the picture. 'The man in the picture is wearing a ring,' she said slowly.

Abdul nodded. He passed her his magnifying glass. 'It's not possible to make out the detail in the drawing, Ellie, but as you can see the ring appears to be similar to the one in the dead man's canoe – certainly from that period.'

'May I see the ring?' said Dad.

Abdul passed it across.

'Look!' cried Kal. 'What's that?'

A large boat with a strange triangular sail had come into view beyond the reef.

'Wonderful!' cried Faru. 'It's one of the big dhows from the Persian Gulf.'

'We see very few of them these days,' said Abdul. 'What a marvellous sight! Do you realise, that design has hardly changed in two thousand years?'

They watched as the dhow sailed towards them. It seemed to be heading straight for the reef but at the last minute the massive lateen sail changed position, the dhow tacked ponderously round and headed back out to sea.

'Is that what the slaves were taken in?' asked Lucy.

Abdul nodded. 'Exactly that type of ship. That one is probably very old and might even have been used for slaves in the past.'

'Can the dhows get across the reef at high tide?' asked Kal.

'No.' Abdul shook his head.

'So how did they get the slaves on, then?'

'The dhows would have moored in Watumwani creek where there's a break in the reef.'

'But people – authorities and so on – would have seen them,' said Lucy. 'They could have stopped them.'

'Yes, but don't forget, the dhows would also have been conducting lawful trade. If the authorities inspected them, all they would find would be spices, fruit, ivory – that sort of thing. The slaves would then be put on at night and the dhow would sail away under cover of darkness.'

'Dreadful business,' muttered Faru. 'Terrible.'

'It was indeed,' said Abdul. 'Life below decks must have been appalling – probably even worse than in the caves. Many slaves would have died.'

'Horrible,' said Mum.

Kal jumped up and ran to the end of the veranda. He swung Faru's telescope round and lined up on the dhow. 'Come and see,' he called.

They all took turns looking.

'It looks like some writing on the back,' said Lucy, as she squinted through the telescope. 'But I can't read it.'

'May I see?' asked Abdul. He pushed his glasses onto his forehead and peered through the eyepiece. 'It's Arabic and hard to make out but...' He gave a sharp intake of breath. 'It's called the Suleiman Sulman.'

'Sulman's boat?' whispered Ellie.

'Very possibly.'

They watched the dhow until it disappeared round a headland then turned their attention back to the ring.

'Any thoughts, David?' asked Craig.

'Well I…'

'Can that wait, Dad?' cried Lucy. 'I think we should take Abdul to the forest before it gets too late. We can talk about the ring later.'

'Good idea,' said Faru. 'I'd also like to come and see what young Kal has discovered.'

'And I'm going to show you that path,' said Lucy.

CHAPTER 17

Baobab tree

THE RUIN

Kal drove. Lucy sat in the front between him and Craig, with Fupi on her lap. Faru and Abdul travelled in the seat behind. The others stayed at the house.

'Over there,' said Craig, when they reached the field, 'by the baobab.'

'What's a baobab?' asked Lucy.

'That's what the tree's called,' said Craig.

'Very old, that one,' said Faru, 'hundreds, possibly thousands, of years.'

'Looks like it's growing upside down,' said Kal.

'That's the hyena's fault,' said Faru with a chuckle.

'The what?'

'Apparently the hyena wasn't paying attention when God handed out the trees for the animals to plant,' said Faru, 'and he planted his the wrong way up.'

'Who says?'

'Old folk tale – one of many.'

'Huh,' muttered Kal, as he stopped the Land Rover by the gap in the fence.

'You lot have made a right mess,' said Lucy.

'Sorry about that,' said Craig, 'but is this where your path came out?'

'It was about here. There aren't any other big trees like that.' She peered at the creepers and bushes. 'I know everything looks a bit overgrown but I'm certain it's here.'

Kal drove through the gap to the inner forest. The others followed on foot, and although they searched for some ten minutes, could find no sign of a path.

'Are you sure this is the right place?' said Faru.

Lucy scowled and said nothing.

'What about the building you found?' asked Abdul.

'Over there,' said Craig. 'Let's walk; it's only a short way.'

They set off, with Fupi trotting in front sniffing the unfamiliar coastal smells.

'Stop!' hissed Lucy, and pointed.

The elephant-shrew was snuffling through the leaves with its long snout. They kept very still and it came quite close. Fupi whined. The elephant-shrew gave a squeak and scampered off to some thick bushes.

'That's where the building is,' said Kal.

Lucy felt a knot in her tummy as they got closer. They were approaching what might have been a building at one time but it was now a ruin almost hidden by creepers. But that doorway – it was the same! Except it wasn't; it was now collapsed and a tree was growing out of the middle. Lucy shivered.

'So the local tales are true,' muttered Faru.

'Yes, yes,' cried Abdul, 'absolutely.' He hurried forward.

'Watch out for snakes,' called Craig.

Abdul stopped. 'We must do this properly,' he said. 'We can look round now, but I will need to return with my equipment and carry out a proper survey.'

'That could be another building over there,' said Faru, pointing to some other bushes.

'And there!' cried Kal. 'But it's all so overgrown.'

'And that could be another,' said Craig.

'Let's see if we can find some more,' said Kal, setting off.

Now they knew what to look for, it soon became apparent that they were in the middle of a ruined settlement but one that was completely overgrown with forest creepers, plants and trees, and clearly totally deserted.

'This is really extraordinary,' cried Abdul. 'There is no question that this is an old Arab village – and not yet mapped.'

Craig drew Lucy aside. 'Is this the place?' he whispered.

She nodded. 'Craig, it's so scary. It wasn't overgrown like this. It was all open. Okay, the houses looked old but they were…' She froze. 'He's there,' she whispered, 'by that old building where the elephant-shrew went.'

Craig put a hand on her shoulder. 'There's no one, Lucy. It's just…'

There was a sudden scream.

They whirled round.

Kal had disappeared.

All they could see was a hole in the ground with a few leaves fluttering into it.

CHAPTER 18

Cicada

THE REEF

Lucy picked up the echo of Kal's scream with her own.

Craig raced over to the hole and threw himself down at the edge. 'Kal!' he yelled. There was no reply. 'Kal!' He looked round. 'Faru, is there a torch in the Landy?'

'Yes, in the front glove compartment. I'll go and...'

Craig jumped up. 'I'll go.' He set off at a run.

Lucy lay down and peered into the hole. 'Kal,' she called. Her voice echoed off the walls of a shaft leading to impenetrable darkness. Her head slumped to the ground.

The sound of the cicadas was deafening in the oppressive forest. Lucy tried to shut out the cacophony of their noise and listen for sounds coming from the shaft. She called again and thought she could hear the sound of water sloshing but there was no answering call. She buried her face in her hands. 'Kal,' she whimpered.

Fupi growled, but Lucy didn't look up and didn't see the old man in the turban and the *kanzu* who was watching her.

Kal tried to scream. He couldn't. He couldn't breathe. He was suffocating. No, he wasn't! *He was drowning!*

He kicked wildly with his legs, his head came clear of the water and he sucked in great lungfuls of beautiful air.

He looked frantically around. It was completely dark. His hand came against a slippery rock. He tried to grab it but his body was dragged away. He lunged again into the darkness. His fingers scrabbled on the slippery surface of another rock. The invisible force pulled him back under the water. He heard screams. Impossible – you're under water. More screams. His whole head was filling with screaming – agonising desperate screaming.

His head came out of the water. He snatched a mouthful of air. Again he was sucked down. Again the screaming. His head was bursting.

I'm going to die.

The salt water stung his eyes. Everywhere was completely black. *I'm going to die.* No! He blinked to clear the saltiness. There *was* some light. There, far away under the water – a faint bluish light. And he was being sucked towards it.

He fought his way to the surface again and snatched a quick breath before being sucked down again. He couldn't fight it any longer. He twisted his body and dived towards the light.

His lungs screamed for air, his head was filled with screaming, his whole body was screaming. His speed increased. The light was getting brighter. He was almost there. The light was blinding. He was almost in heaven.

He shot into the sunlight.

He lay back and closed his eyes, letting his lungs take over, while he was buoyed along on the gentle current.

The screaming had stopped.

Craig was back. He was panting and sweat was soaking through his shirt. He threw himself down beside Lucy and shone the torch. 'Kal!' he yelled.

Still no answer.

The torchlight reflected off the sides of a narrow shaft, the walls of which were covered in greenish slime. After about three metres, the shaft turned a corner and they could see no further.

'Craig, there's no answer,' wailed Lucy, 'only water sloshing.'

'I'll get a rope,' cried Faru. 'But it'll mean going back to the house.'

'The keys are in the ignition,' shouted Craig, as Faru ran off.

'Please be quick,' called Lucy.

'The walls are completely smooth,' muttered Craig, examining the hole. 'This has got to be man-made.'

'But who by?' asked Lucy.

'Slave-traders,' said Abdul quietly. 'I think this is a shaft leading to one of those caves where slaves were imprisoned, and this was the way they got them in.'

Lucy gulped. Could it be the underwater cave that she and Kal had discovered?

'I guess you're right, Abdul,' said Craig, continuing his examination. 'See, there are the remains of some iron brackets round the edge.'

'There was probably a metal grill over the top, which has rusted away,' said Abdul, 'and Kal was unlucky enough to step on the place hidden under the leaves.'

'Kal,' whimpered Lucy, and her head slumped forward again.

Craig's face was full of concern. 'Faru will be as quick as he can.'

The cicadas suddenly stopped calling and the forest fell ominously silent.

A shiver ran down Lucy's back.

The water was beautifully warm and the current bore Kal effortlessly along – carrying him away from the cave and allowing him to collect his thoughts. That had to be the cave that he and Lucy had explored yesterday morning, where they found the skeleton – the skeleton with one arm. Was it only yesterday? So much seemed to have happened since... One arm! His eyes snapped open. That was it! He knew there had been something odd; the skeleton had only one arm. He lay back in the warm water. So what?

He gazed into the blue sky overhead, enjoying the sensation of being buoyed up by the soothing warm water and free of that dreadful screaming. The current seemed to be moving faster. He turned his head lazily to one side.

All thoughts of one-armed skeletons vanished.

The current that had sucked him out of the cave was now dragging him, not into some tranquil lagoon, but towards the deadly reef, perhaps even out to Shark Island!

He thrashed in panic. The only thing he achieved was exhausting himself.

Think!

His pace increased. The reef was getting nearer. The pounding of the surf was getting louder. He had a glimpse of a break in the reef: that *mlango* place where the currents were even stronger and where sharks lurked. He fought down the panic and forced himself to stop battling against the current.

Sideways. That was it! Swim sideways across the current.

He struck out powerfully. Very quickly the current slackened.

A few more strokes and he was clear of the relentless pull. The water all around looked calm and peaceful. There was no sign of that force that could so easily have swept him to... He shut his mind to the thought, turned his back on the pounding reef and set off with a measured breaststroke towards the beach.

He reached the shallows, waded out of the water, up the beach and back towards the house. He hurried up the steep path to the veranda and could hear voices, laughter and the chink of crockery. The others must have started lunch. Thank goodness they hadn't heard about the near disaster. He avoided the front of the house and ran round to the back, and there was Faru's Land Rover. He reached it just as Faru emerged from a shed, carrying a rope.

Faru's mouth dropped open and the rope fell to the ground. 'Bless my soul,' he muttered.

'It's okay, Faru,' said Kal, 'I'm all right.'

'What... how...?'

'I fell into a cave that connects with the sea and got pulled out by the tide.'

'Good Lord! And you're not hurt?'

'A bit bruised and scratched, but I'm fine.'

'Thank goodness! The others are worried sick. They're still waiting at the... Jump in!' Faru left the rope on the ground, leapt into the driver's seat of the vehicle and shot off before Kal even had the chance to close his door. Faru hit a rut and the vehicle bounced into the air.

Kal grabbed at the door and tried to hang on.

'I used to drive in the Safari Rally,' shouted Faru, swerving skilfully round a pothole. 'When it was just locals.' He corrected a skid. 'First African driver to finish.' He squeezed between two fence posts. They had now reached the field. Faru changed gear and put his foot to the floor and the vehicle sped over the smooth grass. He changed down when they reached the gap in the fence but barely slackened his pace. He narrowly missed the great trunk of the baobab tree and they shot almost blindfold into the forest. He drifted expertly round another tree that approached at alarming speed. The vehicle hit a hole, bounced up and slewed sideways. Faru threw the wheel over, straightened up and flattened a bush.

'Faru!' yelled Kal.

'What?'

'We're nearly there!'

Faru slowed down. 'So we are.'

By the time they reached the others, Faru was travelling at a sedate pace. He pulled up and switched off the engine. He turned and winked at Kal. 'Haven't had so much fun in years,' he chuckled.

'That was awesome,' said Kal.

Faru harrumphed awkwardly. 'So glad you're safe.'

Did he mean safe from the cave or from the ride, wondered Kal?

CHAPTER 19

Man wearing a kanzu

THE ONE-ARMED MAN

'It was the cave that Lucy and I found,' said Kal, as Faru drove everyone back through the forest, 'when we went exploring yesterday morning.'

'We think it was one of those caves you were telling us about, Abdul,' said Lucy. 'There's iron rings and things hammered into the rock.'

'Goodness!' cried Abdul. 'It sounds a terrible place.'

'It is.'

'Almost certainly a cave that was used for slaves,' he said.

'And that shaft Kal fell down, connects with it?' said Faru.

'Yeah,' said Kal. 'We saw this hole high up in the wall. I guess that's where I came through. Good job the tide was in.'

'You could have been…!'

'Okay, okay, Lucy.'

'And there's a skeleton there, you told me?' said Craig.

'A skeleton!' cried Abdul.

Lucy looked down at her hands. 'It was horrible,' she muttered.

'We reckoned the guy had been chained up,' said Kal, 'but there was something odd about him. I've now realised what it was. He had only one arm.'

'What?' exclaimed Lucy and Abdul, together.

'It was… What is it, Abdul?' cried Kal.

Abdul was furiously polishing his glasses and looking agitated. 'I just need to check something when we get back.'

They came clear of the forest and headed towards the house.

'Can we, er… not say too much about all this?' said Kal. 'About my falling into that hole and things. Mum would freak out.'

Faru nodded. 'No sense in alarming them. We'll have to tell the police, though, about the skeleton, but the poor fellow has probably been in the cave for years, so another day or so won't matter.'

⁂

'Sorry we didn't wait for you,' called Diana, when they reached the house to find the others, except for Dad, sitting round the lunch table. 'We were all feeling a bit peckish.'

'What did you find?' asked Ellie.

'Most exciting,' cried Abdul. 'There is an undoubted Arab settlement in the forest, which could be an important archaeological site.'

'Is it very old?' asked Mum.

'Probably built sometime during the fourteenth or fifteenth century.'

'Fascinating place,' said Faru. 'To think, it's been there all this time and I never realised.'

Abdul nodded. 'Once these sites fall into decline, the forest invades very quickly, as we saw.'

'Kal!' exclaimed Mum. 'What on earth happened to you? You're filthy and your T-shirt is all torn.'

'He tripped over and caught it on a branch,' said Craig hastily.

'Most unfortunate,' said Faru.

'Really, Kal,' said Mum, 'you ought to take more care. That was a present from Granny.'

'Sorry, Mum.'

'Did you find your path, Lucy?' asked Ellie.

'Rather,' said Faru, cutting in. 'Very clear. Quite obvious. Can't understand how we could have missed it.'

Lucy had to put her head down so that the others couldn't see the smile.

'Was that man there?' asked Mum. 'The one who showed Lucy the path?'

'No, no sign,' said Faru.

'Who do you think that was, Faru?' asked Diana.

'No idea. Probably some fisherman.' He gave a brief chuckle. 'Obviously knows his way round the reserve better than I do.'

Lucy glanced at Craig, who gave a slight smile and winked. She didn't dare look at Kal, who had his hand over his mouth. 'Where's Dad?' she asked.

'He has an important scientific paper he wants to finish,' said Mum. 'You know how engrossed he can...'

'Any lunch left?' called a voice, and Dad appeared from inside the house.

'Yes, but we were just about to clear...' Ellie's voice trailed off. 'What on earth is that you're wearing?'

'Dad, it's a skirt!' cried Kal.

'If you must know, it's called a *kikoi*,' said Dad loftily.

'Everyone wears them at the coast. Now, if you'll excuse me, I'm right in the middle of the conclusions.' He reached across the table to the fruit bowl. 'Going really well,' he said, brandishing a banana and hurrying back inside.

'Mum,' said Ellie, 'did you put Dad up to that?'

'I think he looks very nice,' said Mum. 'It's just the thing for this hot climate. I've also bought one for Kal.'

Kal's jaw dropped open. 'You what?'

'While Ellie was here studying Abdul's book and the rest of you were out, Diana and I went with Hannah to the local market.'

'You've bought me a skirt?' said Kal, a note of incredulity in his voice.

'Yes, dear, a very nice one.'

'Right,' said Kal, glaring at Mum, 'you're expecting me to wear a skirt.'

'Do stop making such a fuss, Kal. The colours will suit you very well. And we bought *kangas* for the girls,' she added, before Kal could think of a suitable retort.

'Where?' cried Ellie. 'Can we see them?'

'Not just now, dear, I think Abdul might want to tell us something more about the book.'

'What, Abdul?' cried Lucy. 'Something about Mahmoud Omar?'

Abdul pushed away the book that he had been studying and peered over the top of his glasses at each of them in turn, a slight smile on his lips. Then he rested his chin on his hands and gazed out to sea.

The others waited for him to speak.

'It all makes sense,' he murmured.

'What does? What do you mean?' asked Lucy.

Abdul turned away from the view and looked round the table. 'Another piece has been fitted into the jigsaw puzzle.'

'What? Tell us!'

'I will, Lucy, but first let's hear what Ellie discovered.' He passed the book over to her and smiled encouragingly. 'Tell us what you learned.'

Ellie took a deep breath. 'There's quite a lot about Mahmoud Omar,' she said, indicating the woodcut print of the old man. 'He was not a slave trader, but he was closely involved in the trade.'

'How?' asked Lucy.

'He found out where captured slaves were being held in caves and other places, and then released them.'

'Bet the slave traders got pretty hacked off,' said Kal.

Abdul nodded. 'It would have taken a lot of courage. Unfortunately, it cost him his life. Tell them, Ellie.'

'No one knows for sure what happened,' she said, turning the pages, 'but it appears that Omar was given a tip-off about some slaves being held in a cave at Watumwani.'

'A cave here?' said Mum.

'Yes,' said Abdul. It was his turn to conceal a smile. 'Must be somewhere near here.'

Lucy and Kal glanced at each other.

'Omar went to this cave,' said Ellie, 'but when he got there he didn't find slaves chained to the walls – only slave traders, and they waiting for him.'

'He was set up?' cried Kal.

'Yes. He was captured, chained up and left.'

'Poor fellow,' muttered Faru.

Everyone was quiet for a moment.

'Ellie, show us the picture again?' said Abdul. 'Kal, do you notice anything, anything odd about that man – something we missed earlier?'

Kal looked. 'No I...' Then he turned pale. 'He's lost an arm,' he whispered.

Abdul nodded, studied his hands for a moment and then looked up. 'Mahmoud Omar's real name was Suleiman Sulman.'

'Omar and Sulman are the same person?' cried Kal.

'Undoubtedly.'

'So that skeleton in the cave is…'

'Skeleton!' cried Mum. 'What skeleton?'

'I guess it's something I must have read,' muttered Kal.

Lucy made a face at Kal. That was close.

Abdul gave a brief smile. 'It seems that Sulman changed his name to Mahmoud Omar when he renounced the slave trade after the incident with the lions.'

'That time he lost his arm and was rescued by Punyura, Punyua – whatever his name was?' said Kal.

Adbul nodded. 'I think Sulman was so ashamed of being a slave trader that he wanted to start a new life with a new name.' He looked round the group. 'So – it seems I no longer have to feel guilty about my ancestor.'

'Certainly not,' said Faru. 'You can be very proud.' He nodded and stroked his chin. 'So, does that complete the puzzle?'

Abdul looked pensive. 'Well, almost, but there are still a few… ' His voice trailed off. The others waited, but he remained lost in thought.

Lucy reached for the book and studied the picture. It looked so like the man who had led her through the forest, and whom she had seen in the cave. But that was probably because he was wearing the same kind of clothes. Could he have been an ancestor, she wondered? Or could the man she'd seen have been his… his ghost? Despite the heat of the day, she couldn't help a shiver running through her body.

She bent down and scooped up Fupi. 'We're off to the beach,' she said.

CHAPTER 20

Coconut palms

GHOSTS

Lucy wanted time to think. She sat in the shade of a coconut palm, her knees drawn up and her chin resting on them as she watched Kal and Ellie who had just set off snorkelling over the coral. Fupi sat next to her gazing warily at the ghost crabs scuttling back and forth. Lucy stroked the little dog. 'Can you understand what it all means?' she whispered.

Fupi wagged her tail then pricked her ears. Craig had come onto the beach. 'Hi,' he said, as he settled beside them.

'Hi.' Lucy smiled and continued to gaze out to sea. 'Craig,' she said, after a while, 'do you think I'm mad?'

'No.' He glanced at her and shook his head. 'You're not mad, Lucy. No way.'

'But why do I keep seeing that man? No one else sees him.'

'Matata might have done.'

Lucy nodded. 'But no one else does.'

'Perhaps he slips away as soon as he realises someone has spotted him.'

'You don't really think that – do you?'

Craig was watching the crabs and didn't reply.

'Craig, what is it?'

'Lucy, I think you might be sensitive to things that the rest of us aren't.'

'So you're saying I *am* mad.'

'No.'

'What, then – bonkers, nutty, screwy? It's all the same!'

Craig took a deep breath.

'Sorry.' She started drawing aimlessly in the sand.

They were silent for a moment as they watched Ellie and Kal.

'Mum always says I'm the sensitive one,' said Lucy. 'Am I?'

Craig smiled. 'On the surface, no; but underneath, yes.'

There was a cry from Kal, who was waving. They couldn't hear what he said, so just waved back.

'Craig, that ring.'

'Uh huh.'

'The man in the picture: Omar, Sulman – whatever we call him – was wearing a ring.'

Craig nodded.

'But the man I saw in the forest, wasn't. I would have noticed.'

'So?'

'I don't know.' Lucy continued drawing in the sand. 'Craig, who is he?'

'Omar's ghost?'

'I don't believe in ghosts.'

Craig smiled. 'I don't suppose you do.'

Lucy stopped her drawing and looked out to sea. 'At least, I don't think I do,' she murmured.

They were both silent for a while. 'Is it the same man as Matata saw?' she asked.

'Who knows? Whoever, or whatever, it was, scared him big time.'

'The man didn't scare me,' said Lucy. 'He just seemed friendly.'

Craig nodded. 'Don't forget, Lucy, although you may not believe in ghosts, Matata almost certainly does. Such things would play an important part in his life.'

'Like when he was living alone in the forest, you mean – before we rescued him?'

'Yes. So, if he sees someone who apparently disappears, he'll immediately think of ghosts or spirits.'

'Could it have been the same for the man in the canoe – the one who died?'

'I guess so. We know the people at the coast can be very superstitious.'

'He certainly looked as though he'd seen a ghost.'

'Perhaps he saw something in the cave.'

'That old man was in the cave,' said Lucy. 'I saw him when Kal and I went exploring. Perhaps there's a way in, other than the shaft, that we don't know about.'

Craig shrugged.

'You're not convinced.'

'No.' Craig looked thoughtful. 'You know, Lucy, one explanation could be…'

'Hi,' called Kal.

He and Ellie were coming up the beach carrying their flippers and facemasks. Fupi stood up and wagged her tail.

'Good session?' asked Craig.

'It's really cool,' said Kal.

'You two are looking very serious,' said Ellie, as she and Kal settled down beside them.

'We're trying to make sense out of all this,' said Lucy. 'Kal, have you told Ellie about the cave?'

'Yeah.'

'I'm glad I wasn't with you,' said Ellie. 'Have you told Mum or Dad?'

'No way!' cried Lucy. 'Mum would really freak out if she knew.'

'That guy in the canoe looked pretty freaked out,' said Kal.

'We were just talking about him,' said Lucy. 'We wondered whether he might have seen something in the cave.'

'Like what?' asked Ellie.

'Like... like... I don't know.'

'Kal,' said Ellie, 'when you fell into the cave did you see anything?'

'You've got to be joking,' said Kal. 'It was pitch-black. All I was trying to do was survive.'

'I've never seen anyone look so terrified as the man in the canoe,' said Lucy. 'He must have seen *something*.'

'Or heard something,' murmured Kal.

They all stared at him.

'I know it seems stupid,' he said, 'but when I was in the water, I heard screaming.'

'Screaming?' said Lucy.

'Yeah, like my head was going to burst.'

'It wasn't anoxia?' said Craig.

'What's that?'

'When your brain gets starved of oxygen. That can cause pounding in the head.'

Kal shook his head. 'No, it was screaming – really freaky screaming. Much more of it, and *my* brain would have fried.'

'It doesn't make sense,' said Lucy.

'I think it could,' said Craig quietly.

'What do you mean?'

Craig paused for a moment. 'Listen, guys, let's forget what we understand, what we think of as normal, and come at this another way.'

'How?' said Kal.

'It all seems to link to the cave,' said Craig, 'a cave where the most terrible things have happened – slaves imprisoned, that guy chained up and left to die, people going there and coming out mad, and Lucy seeing things, and Kal hearing things.'

'I read somewhere that when something awful happens, like a murder or a violent death,' said Ellie, 'it creates so much energy it affects the molecules in buildings and places, and they become haunted.'

'Are you saying that's what ghosts are?' said Kal.

Ellie shrugged.

'Don't see how,' said Lucy.

'Nor do I,' said Ellie, 'It's just a theory, but is that what you're suggesting, Craig?'

Craig nodded. 'I guess it is – something like that, anyway. The cave has certainly seen its share of violent death.'

'And all that energy is still there?'

'At least it's an explanation, even if it doesn't add up.'

'And that's what killed the guy in the canoe?' said Kal.

'Possibly.' Craig looked from one to another. 'I think he stole Omar's ring.'

Lucy's eyes widened. 'He took the ring from the skeleton?' she whispered.

'Yes.' Craig stood up. 'Let's go back and join the others.'

When they got back to the veranda, Dad and Abdul were engrossed in discussion, the ring lying on the table in front of them.

Dad looked up. 'You'll be pleased to know I've finished the paper. Some really important conclusions, which, if I'm not mistaken, could change current thinking on...'

'What about the ring, Dad,' asked Lucy.

'Ah, the ring.' Dad held it up as though it were a geological specimen that he was demonstrating to a class of students. 'Firstly, I believe that the metal is gold.'

'So it's valuable?' said Lucy.

'Undoubtedly. But I believe that its real value lies in the stone.'

'Is it ruby?' asked Ellie.

'Almost certainly.'

Faru nodded. 'Didn't the inscription in one of the caves say something about Sulman becoming a rich man?'

'Yes.' Abdul's eyes were shining behind his glasses. 'Please continue, David, I find this fascinating.'

Dad beamed at him. 'The stone is of interest for a number of reasons: firstly, the lapidarist who...'

'What's a lapida-whatsit?' asked Kal.

'Someone who collects butterflies,' said Lucy, 'but what's that got to do with...?'

'A lapidarist, has nothing to do with butterflies,' said Dad, through gritted teeth.

'That's a lepidopterist,' said Ellie. 'A lapidarist is someone who cuts stones and gems.'

'Oh,' said Lucy.

'If you don't mind, Ellie, I am the one who is doing the explaining,' said Dad.

'I was just thinking...'

'Thank you, Ellie. Perhaps you would allow me to continue.'

Ellie and Lucy started to giggle.

'The stone has been cut in a most interesting way,' continued Dad, ignoring the children and addressing his remarks to Abdul, 'but what I find fascinating is the asterism that you may have noticed.'

'The asterism, or star, you mean?' said Abdul.

'Precisely. The presence of rutile needles (probably titanium dioxide) in the uncut gemstone was undoubtedly noticed by the lapidarist who has used these inclusions to great effect when cutting the stone to create the illusion of a star inside it.' He passed the ring to Abdul, who tilted it in the sunlight, and they could all see the star winking from within.

'You may pass it round,' said Dad.

'Fascinating,' said Faru. 'See that?' He passed the ring to Diana.

'It's beautiful,' she said.

'Sulman said he was following a star,' said Ellie.

'Aldebaran, the Follower,' said Faru. 'Rather appropriate for Sulman to honour the star in that way, I'd have thought.'

'A kind of thank you,' said Lucy.

'Yes, it probably was,' said Abdul, now smiling.

'As I was saying before we got side-tracked,' interrupted Dad, 'the presence of inclusions within a stone, can often indicate the source of the material.'

'Do you mean these… these, what you call inclusions, Dad, can tell you where the stone came from?' said Ellie.

'Yes, an expert can often tell you that.'

'So where did this one come from?' asked Kal.

'Well, I am of course, no expert,' said Dad, giving a little chuckle, 'and one would need the appropriate equipment to conduct a proper examination, but I think this stone may have originated from the same source as the ones I have previously examined.'

'From Simba!' cried Lucy.

Dad nodded.

'Bless my soul!' exclaimed Faru.

Craig shook his head. 'To think, if we hadn't had to make that forced landing, none of this would have come to light.'

'Anything else, David?' asked Faru.

'Those are the main points of interest, but the cut of the stone is perhaps unusual.'

'How?'

'The stone is cut *en cabochon* – as the French would say – a dome shape. That is of course to be expected since it would enhance the asterism. But what is unusual is the pendeloque form that the lapidarist has given the stone.'

'What's a bend-a-lot form?' asked Kal.

Dad gave an exasperated sniff. 'Pendeloque, means pear- or drop-shaped.'

'Tear-shaped?' suggested Ellie.

Dad shrugged. 'If you like.'

'*The Follower led me to the tomb, and from here I found where his tears had fallen, and became a rich man,*' quoted Ellie.

Everyone's gaze turned towards her.

Ellie blushed. 'Perhaps "his tears" refers to the stones he found near the cave,' she said, 'and those are what made him rich. Could that be right, Abdul?'

Abdul took off his spectacles and polished them before replying. 'Ellie, that is undoubtedly correct,' he said softly.

'Darling, you are clever,' said Mum.

'Rather,' said Faru.

'And you could say that the tears of the Follower are red because the star itself is red. It all makes sense,' added Ellie.

Everyone began talking at once as they passed the ring around the table, marvelling at its beauty and the wonder of its origin.

Abdul sat back in his chair. 'This has been a most moving experience. I can't say how exciting it has all been.'

'Is it all sorted now?' asked Kal.

'Yes, I suppose it is. But there is one thing. I just wonder...'

'Where the treasure is,' cried Lucy.

'What treasure?' said Kal.

'I know that ring's valuable, but one ring is hardly going to make Sulman a rich man,' said Lucy. 'I bet his real treasure is hidden somewhere.'

'You and your treasure,' muttered Kal.

Abdul chuckled. 'I'm sure there was more to Sulman's riches than just the ring, but I doubt we'll ever know. But that wasn't what I was about to say.' He rummaged in his briefcase and pulled out a note. 'Here we are. This, Craig, is the message you copied from the second cave.'

Craig nodded. 'I tried to be accurate.'

'You've done it very well,' said Abdul. 'The whole thing is perfectly legible.'

'So what's the problem?' asked Lucy.

'I'm just not sure of my translation. Sometimes a term used in the early scripts can be a bit obscure, and one has to make an informed guess.'

'Like what?' said Ellie.

'You remember what it says.' Abdul pushed his spectacles up his nose and scrutinised the text. '*The Follower led me to the tomb, and from here...* et cetera, et cetera.'

Ellie watched Abdul's finger as he moved it along the text. 'What's the bit you're not sure about?'

'This bit.' Abdul pointed. 'I have assumed that the writer is talking about a tomb. It's the nearest approximation I can make to what is actually written.'

'What is written?'

'What it says is: *The Follower led me to the place of the skull.* I have assumed he meant a...'

'What!' cried Lucy.

Abdul's voice trailed off. 'Is something the matter?'

'The Place of the Skull is on Simba ranch,' said Craig slowly. 'It's where the rubies occur.'

'Well, I'm blowed!' cried Faru.

'It's called that because there are some caves in the cliff face that look like the eye sockets and mouth of a skull,' said Ellie.

'We thought it was Matata's dad who gave the place that name,' said Lucy.

'But it wasn't him. It was Sulman!' cried Kal.

'And the name has survived,' said Craig.

'To think that so much history could be wrapped up in that ring,' said Diana.

'Who said history was dull?' cried Lucy.

CHAPTER 21

Millipede

RETURNING THE RING

'What's going to happen to the ring?' asked Kal.

'Should we take it to the police? asked Mum.

'I don't think so,' said Faru. 'They wouldn't thank us for giving them extra paperwork and they wouldn't know what to do with it afterwards.'

'I think Abdul should keep it,' said Diana, 'after all, it did belong to his ancestor.'

Abdul shook his head vigorously. 'No, no, certainly not. If anything, it should go into the museum in Dar es Salaam.'

Faru nodded. 'Good idea – preserve it for the nation.'

'I think we should give it back,' said Lucy.

Everyone stared at her.

'Right,' said Kal, 'I'll just call up Dr Who so we can go back in time in the Tardis and drop it off.'

'Don't be stupid, Kal.'

'What, then?'

'I don't know.'

'I think Lucy's right,' murmured Ellie. She picked up the ring and laid it in the palm of her hand. The star inside twinkled in the bright sunlight. 'It should go back to Sulman. I think he's being tormented by its loss.'

'What's that supposed to mean?' asked Kal.

Ellie shrugged. 'There's a lot of strange things happening, which seem to be linked to the ring.'

'So how do we return it?'

'I have a suggestion,' said Faru, stroking his chin. 'We need to go back to the forest to cover over that hole...'

'Hole? What hole?' said Mum.

'Er, well yes, there's a um... dangerous hole there. Wouldn't want anyone falling in.'

Kal hid his smile.

'Thing is,' continued Faru, 'we could, er... sort of build a cairn at the same time, by that old house. A kind of memorial, as it were, to Sulman, and...'

'And put the ring inside?' cried Lucy.

'Something like that. What do you think, Abdul?'

Abdul looked moved. 'Thank you, Faru. I think that would be most appropriate.'

'I think that's brilliant,' cried Lucy.

Craig picked up the ring and stood up. 'Come on, then. What are we waiting for?'

'I'm coming as well, this time,' said Ellie. 'I want to see the place.'

Half an hour later, the children, together with Craig, Faru and Abdul, were back in the forest with Fupi, who was now getting used to the coastal smells. Lucy glanced round apprehensively. Nothing abnormal. Beautiful turquoise and black swallowtail butterflies flitted through the dappled shade, and a flock of birds moved through the trees overhead. Craig pointed them out to Lucy. 'Take a look; they're rather special.'

Lucy focused her binoculars. 'What are they?'

'Chestnut-fronted helmet-shrikes – a coast speciality.'

'Kal would say you'd made up that name.'

Craig laughed. 'They get it from the chestnut patch just above the beak and the strange crest on the head.'

'Are they rare?'

'Quite.'

She and Craig followed them a short way through the trees.

'Craig, am I being silly?' she asked, when they were out of earshot of the others.

He shook his head.

'Should we return the ring?'

'You won't be happy unless you do, will you?'

Lucy looked at him and smiled. 'No, no I won't.' She paused. 'Nor will that man.'

Craig smiled back. 'Let's go and join the others.'

'Our friend's come to watch,' called Kal, who was heaving the first of two buckets out of the back of the Land Rover.

Lucy wasn't quite sure what she would see. But it was only the elephant-shrew whiffling his nose in their direction. There was no sign of Mahmoud Omar, Suleiman Sulman, or whoever. Lucy felt relieved. It was going to be an ordinary sort of afternoon in the forest, doing ordinary sorts of jobs. She went to help Ellie, Abdul and Faru who were finding pieces of old coral rock with which to make the cairn.

'Just watch out for snakes and scorpions,' warned Faru.

Ellie squawked and jumped back as a large dark brown creature wriggled out from under the rock she had just moved.

'He's all right,' said Faru, 'that's just a *jongololo*, Tanganyika train.'

'A what?'

'Millipede, Tanganyika train – old colonial name.'

'But he's enormous! He must be at least fifteen centimetres long.'

'Yes, but quite harmless. They chew up the leaf litter – jolly good for the soil.'

Fupi went and sniffed it.

'Where shall we have the cairn?' called Kal.

'Over there,' said Lucy. 'Near the remains of the house.'

'Just the place,' said Abdul.

Kal dragged over the buckets, which contained dry sand and cement, tipped the contents onto the ground, went back to the Land Rover for a jerry can of water and a spade, and started to prepare the mixture.

Lucy and Ellie helped the men put the coral rocks in place, and Kal added dollops of cement mixture. Lucy also kept half an eye on the elephant-shrew. At first it seemed interested in what they were doing but it soon disappeared.

After about half an hour, the cairn stood nearly a metre high, and Faru called a halt. Sweat poured off them and they were breathing heavily in the oppressive heat of the forest.

'That is really splendid,' said Abdul. 'All we need now, Kal, is a smooth area on the top.'

Kal scooped up the last of the cement and smoothed it out. 'There we go.'

Lucy ran back to the Land Rover and returned with the ring. She held it up to the light. The star within the ruby glinted in the bright light. She took a deep breath and pushed the ring into the soft cement.

Kal pressed a flat piece of rock on top. 'That's it, then.'

'I suppose we should say a sort of prayer or something,' said

Lucy, 'but I can't think of anything – except thank you.' She sniffed. 'Thanks, Sulman, Omar, whatever your name is. Good luck.'

'*Asante* – thank you,' said Faru, clearing his throat.

'Well done,' said Craig.

Abdul murmured something in Arabic and stood quietly for a moment with his head bowed and his eyes closed.

Lucy blinked and swallowed then looked up at a rustling sound. The elephant-shrew was back. They all stood very still. The little animal came almost up to the cairn, its nose questing forwards. Then it gave a squeak of alarm and scampered off.

'Thank you,' said Abdul. 'Very moving. Thank you everyone.'

'That'll soon mellow and blend in with the rest of the forest,' said Faru. 'Now, I suppose we should be getting back.'

'We mustn't forget about the hole,' said Craig.

'Gracious me, I quite forgot,' said Faru with a chuckle. 'Don't want any more accidents. Nearly put my foot in it, there.'

He and Kal dragged a roll of wire netting out of the back of the Land Rover, and Craig began to hammer in metal stakes round the edge of the hole.

Fupi started whining.

'What is it, Fupi?' asked Lucy. She reached down to pick up the little dog, but Fupi gave a series of frantic barks and raced off.

'Fupi, come back!'

Fupi stopped. She was now barking even more frantically.

'Fupi, what's the…?'

'What's that noise?' cried Ellie.

There was an ominous rumbling from beneath their feet.

'Run!' yelled Craig, grabbing Lucy and Ellie.

They stumbled clear just in time.

What, seconds earlier had been solid ground, was now a massive gaping hole. The ruined house and the cairn had disappeared.

'Anyone hurt?' cried Craig.

'That was so scary!' cried Ellie.

'I think we're okay,' muttered Faru, who was sitting on the ground nursing a bruised knee.

Abdul retrieved his glasses, which had fallen off.

Fupi trotted back to Lucy wagging her tail uncertainly. Lucy picked her up and hugged her. 'You saved our lives, Fupi. You saved us. You are just so clever.' Fupi licked Lucy's face.

Kal went to the edge of the hole and peered in. 'Looks like the whole cave has collapsed.'

'I guess my hammering set it off,' said Craig. 'It must have been incredibly unstable.'

'And Fupi warned us!' cried Lucy. 'If it hadn't been for her, we could all have been...'

'Doesn't bear thinking about,' muttered Faru.

They stood peering into the hole. The occasional piece of rock was still falling in.

'I think the cave's collapse is a most fitting end to a shameful period of history,' said Abdul, a note of finality in his voice.

'And Sulman now has a proper grave,' said Lucy.

'Indeed. So I don't think we'll need to bother the police,' said Faru.

'Time to go,' said Craig. 'But we will have to return and close the area off.'

They climbed into the Land Rover and headed out of the forest. Lucy turned and looked back. The elephant-shrew had reappeared and was sniffing after them.

CHAPTER 22

Ghost crab

CHRISTMAS TREE

As they approached the house, Diana came to meet them. 'Everything all right?' she asked, seeing their sweaty and dust-covered faces.

'Oh yes,' said Lucy, a bit too hastily.

'Good,' said Diana. 'Now, while you've been away, Sarah and I have had a discussion, and have decided we should have a pre-Christmas party.'

'Great,' said Craig.

Diana smiled. 'Faru, would you be able to organise a Christmas tree?'

'Christmas tree!' cried Lucy. 'Where are we going to find a Christmas tree?'

Faru chuckled. 'Rashid will help.'

Rashid brought his *panga* and joined Faru and the children at the foot of a large coconut tree on the beach.

'Best we can do,' said Faru. He nodded to Rashid, who put

the *panga* between his teeth, shinned up the tree, hacked off half a dozen leaves and some green coconuts, then slid down. He chopped the top off the green coconuts and passed them round.

'Best drink on the coast,' said Faru, as they drank the refreshing nutty liquid.

When they had finished, they dragged the leaves up to the house. Craig and Faru, with the aid of bits of wire and some careful chopping, created the semblance of a tree, which they fixed to the railings of the veranda.

'That's really good,' said Lucy. 'Have you got any decorations, Faru?'

'I'll see what I can find.' Faru disappeared into the house and emerged a few minutes later carrying a cardboard box. 'Let's see what's in here.' He blew the dust off the top and peered inside. 'Hmm, not a lot.'

Lucy inspected the moth-eaten tinsel, the few coloured balls (several of which were broken), and the dubious lights. 'I know,' she cried, 'we should use flowers – bougainvillea, hibiscus and things – that will be much better for a coast Christmas.'

'And shells and bits of coral off the beach,' said Ellie.

'Much better,' agreed Faru. 'But let's see if the lights work. I'll do that. You girls do the artistic parts.'

When they had finished, Lucy called everyone together to admire the tree.

'I think it's lovely, dear,' said Mum.

'That angel looks a bit dodgy,' said Kal.

'That's not an angel. It's a reindeer!' snapped Lucy.

'It's got foot-and-mouth disease.'

'Kal, if you're going to criticise… It's not as though you did anything to help.'

'Come on, guys,' called Craig, who was heading for the beach. 'I need some help to organise the barbecue.'

The last time the children had had a barbecue in Africa was at Simba ranch, in the wonderful setting of the bush, with tall trees around them reflecting the glow of the log fire. This time, the firelight was reflected, not off acacias, but off palm trees, off the waves that lapped gently against the shoreline, and off the eyes of ghost crabs.

Lucy couldn't decide which setting was better. She reached down and tickled Fupi's ears. 'Isn't this so special?' she whispered.

Fupi wagged her tail in agreement.

Lucy, Ellie and Mum wore their new *kangas*. Mum had told the girls not to say anything to Kal who was trying to look cool in his *kikoi*. Lucy felt sure that he was only persuaded because Craig, Dad and Abdul were wearing theirs.

Abdul stood up, looking embarrassed. 'I don't want to interrupt our evening,' he said, 'but I wonder if we might drink a toast to an absent friend. To Suleiman Sulman,' he cried, raising his glass.

They raised and chinked their glasses. 'To Suleiman Sulman.'

Lucy took a sip from her glass and looked along the beach. It was quite dark by the forest where the Sinawe River came out.

'Is that old guy there?' asked Kal, who was watching her.

'No,' she said, wondering if Kal secretly believed what she'd seen. 'He won't be coming back.'

She lay back on the sand and gazed into the heavens. A star with a reddish tinge seemed to be shining even more brightly tonight.

'But I wonder where his treasure is?' she murmured.

If you enjoyed *The Elephant-Shrew*, watch out for the next
African Safari Adventure:

The Buffalo-Weaver

Witchcraft comes to Simba wildlife ranch in Tanzania and Maasai
cattle start dying. Very soon, Lucy, Kal, Ellie, Matata the Maasai
boy, and Fupi the terrier become caught up in this nightmare
which threatens even their lives as they face the terrors of raging
rivers, evil omens, night-time chanting and Devil Buffaloes.

Will the children be able to discover the source of witchcraft?
Even if they do, will they be able to destroy it, before it destroys
the ranch – and them?

Don't buy this book if you are afraid of hippos.

THE SERIES

Everyone who goes to East Africa hopes to see the Big Five: lion, elephant, buffalo, leopard and rhinoceros, but very few are aware of the Little Five, from which the
AFRICAN SAFARI ADVENTURES
take their titles.

If you are lucky enough to be taken on safari, watch out for the Little Five.

The ANT-LION is an insect, the adult of which flies at night. It looks like a damselfly or small dragonfly.

The ELEPHANT-SHREW. Several species occur in East Africa, most of which are the size of large mice. One that occurs in coastal forests is the size of a small dog.

The BUFFALO-WEAVER is a black bird with a red beak, similar in size to a thrush. It nests in colonies, building an untidy nest of sticks.

The LEOPARD-TORTOISE is the most likely of the Little Five to be noticed. It occurs in dry bush and can be recognised by the black blotches on its sandy-coloured shell.

The RHINOCEROS-BEETLE is one of the largest beetles in Africa. Only the male has the large "horn" from which this insect gets its name.